Other books by Wyn Estelle Owens:

But One Life
A Revolutionary Snow White

The Dragon's Flower
An Asian Rapunzel

The Dark King's Curse
A Celtic Twelve Dancing Princesses

Secrets of the Mountain

Wyn Estelle Owens

DEDICATION

To Grandmama, who taught me to love the wild spirit of the North in our blood.

And to Tryg, who lent both his editing services and his name to this book.

May the sea winds always fill your sails!

And, as always, to God: for giving me my talent and the inspiration I need.
Solo Deo Gloria!

CONTENTS

PART 1

CHAPTER 1

S vanhilda always knew when her birthday was coming; the rowans that climbed the mountain's slopes were garlanded with flowers as bright and white as snow.

But now the new baby was coming, and the rowans were burdened with their crowns of bright red fruit instead.

She huffed impatiently, rocking back and forth on her heels, and tugged harshly on one braid. "Papa, when is the baby gonna come? It's been so *long* already!"

Papa laughed, and his large hand settled comfortingly on Svanhilda's head, fingers ruffling the wheat gold locks fondly. "Babies come in their own time, my girl. Have patience! It'll be here when it's ready."

Svanhilda puffed out her cheeks and tugged on her braid again before picking up a stick and distractedly poking the ground with it. He *kept* saying that, and it still hadn't come! Babies were very silly and lazy creatures, she thought.

Her Papa laughed again, patted her head one more time, and returned to his wood carving. Svanhilda poked at the ground with her stick once or twice more, before she scampered over to where he sat beneath the rowan tree, peering curiously over his arm. "What'cha doin', Papa?"

Papa lowered his knife and held up the piece of wood, smiling. It was almost done, the wood carefully etched away into the shape of a kitten.

Svanhilda's eyes widened excitedly. "Kitty!"

"Yes, a kitty," Papa said. Svanhilda reached for it excitedly; Papa held it out of reach, tugging fondly on her braid with his free hand.

"Hold on now, duckling. It's for the new baby."

Svanhilda's big blue eyes bored into her father, filled with such sheer devastation the likes of which the world had never seen. Her father, however, was made of sterner stuff, and merely laughed, tugging on her braid again. "Don't be so sad, now, duckling. The new baby will share with you, just as you'll share your toys with her."

The girl's face twisted up unhappily. "…Don' wanna."

"I'm afraid that whether you want to or not doesn't have much to do with it," Papa said gravely, a smile tugging at the corner of his mouth. "It's just something that a sibling has to learn to do."

Svanhilda looked less than convinced but subsided, returning to poking the ground, dragging the tip of her stick through the grass.

"Getting the pebble ready for the new arrival, eh?" A deep voice rumbled across the clearing, and Svanhilda's head jerked up, her eyes and mouth wide with excitement.

"Granfaffer!"

Grandfather smiled down on the girl, his mouth curving beneath his beard and mustache, his eyes crinkling cheerily. "Well, now, little pebble, come over here and let me see how you've grown!"

Svanhilda immediately dropped her stick and jumped to her feet, scrambling across the clearing and throwing her arms around her grandfather, reaching up a little to squeeze him tightly about the waist.

Only a little, though, for her grandfather was barely over twice her height.

Grandfather burst out laughing, a rough, rumbling sound like stones rolling down a mountain. One of his large, rough hands came down on Svanhilda's head—a warm, familiar weight that made the girl burst out into giggles.

"Well, well, pebble, you've certainly been doing a fair bit of growing. Don't tell me you'll forsake your poor old grandfather to take after some stringy ash tree like Kiúli."

"Hey, now," Kiúli drawled from where he leaned against the rowan tree, not looking up from the whittling in his hands. "That's uncalled for."

"Yeah, what's wrong wif being like Papa?" Svanhilda backed up, pouting.

"Well…" her grandfather said slowly, the twinkle growing in his eyes, "if you get much taller, it'll be hard for me to do… this!" And with that, he swung her up in the air, squealing and giggling, and plonked her down on his shoulder. Svanhilda grabbed ahold of his braids for stability, swaying slightly as she peered about excitedly from her new vantage point. Then, she patted her grandfather on top of his head.

"All-righ', Granfaffer. I'll stay small, jus' for you. Promise!"

"That's very kind of you, pebble," Grandfather said with a smile. He ambled over to where Kiúli sat, Svanhilda giggling as she bounced up and down on his shoulder. When they approached, Kiúli stood up, smiling warmly and bending down to clasp arms with his father-in-law.

"Welcome, Master Alvíss! It's been some time."

"So it has, my lad!" Alvíss replied, before shooting Kiúli a stern glance. "I trust you have been taking good care of my girl?"

"As best I can," Kiúli vowed solemnly.

"That's all I need to hear!" Alvíss replied, and yanked on the younger man's arm, tugging Kiúli down to a height he could reach, and slapped his son-in-law heartily on the back. "Now, how goes the waiting?"

"I thought it would be easier," Kiúli said with a rueful smile, "but I find that it is not."

"Ha! No, it is not, I fear." Alvíss began to sit down, causing Svanhilda to shriek and grab tighter ahold of his braids to keep her balance. "I remember those days very well; the wait is arduous indeed."

"It's takin' *forever,*" Svanhilda informed her grandfather seriously, patting his head for attention.

"You would think," a new voice broke in, deeper and sharper, like flecks of flint rather than the river-smoothed gravel of Alvíss' tone, "that we could have just waited until the whole thing's done, rather than be forced to sit and wait."

Kiúli frowned slightly before the expression was smoothed away under the mask of politeness. Alvíss didn't remove his frown, but it was lighter and more rueful.

"Come now, little brother. Have some patience! Babies take time, you know. Why, you certainly did. I was well old enough to remember when mother labored a day and a little more to bring *you* forth."

His brother snorted and strode over to take his place on a rock beside a neighboring tree. His beard and braids were black, unlike his brother's ruddy brown, but his eyes were the same slate gray. His, though, were narrower and sharper, and they lacked Alvíss' laughter lines.

"Aye, and I've had to sit through every one of your offspring's births, Alvíss, so I believe I've well made up for it," he retorted.

Alvíss rolled his eyes. "Then get yourself a wife, Althjóf, and have a child or two of your own, and that'll teach you the true pain of waiting. Not that it would even shine a candle on the pain your wife would be going through, but it would grant you a little sympathy for us."

"No chance," Althjóf snapped back quickly. "I have more important things."

His elder brother sighed. "Work and craftsmanship are important indeed, and worth dedication, but hoarded gold warms not the heart."

"If gold cannot fetch it, I have little use for it," Althjóf replied, and Alvíss sighed heavily. Svanhilda, not understanding the intricacies of the adult's conversation, squirmed on her grandfather's shoulder. Kiúli, being attentive, reached over and swung his giggling daughter into his lap.

Alvíss turned to the little girl and patted her head, leaning close to her ear and saying quietly, "That's what you'll have to look forward to, my pebble… little siblings will put frost in your hair, mark my words! But they're worth it all the same. There's not a treasure in all my halls nor all the king's hoard that is equal to the gold of kinship and brotherhood… or sisterhood, as the case may be."

Svanhilda didn't quite understand all this, but it seemed important, so she nodded solemnly.

Alvíss returned his gaze to Kiúli, who had finished his carving and was busy ensuring his knife was safely beyond the reach of curious little questing fingers. "Well, I asked before, but never got a proper answer… how fare you with the wait?"

Kiúli smiled ruefully and lifted one shoulder in resignation. "Growing ever-impatient and nursing the sting to my soul that there's nothing I can do to protect her from this pain."

Alvíss nodded sympathetically. "Aye, I remember it well. I had to go through it six times, you know, my lad. How long has Ingiborg been in her travail?"

Kiúli squinted up at the sun thoughtfully through the canopy of the trees, which were already turning the brilliant shades of autumn. "Some five hours now, nearing six. But it might be a long while yet." He sighed restlessly but smiled as he looked down and ruffled Svanhilda's soft flaxen hair. "Svanhilda here kept her mother busy for nearly fifteen hours!"

The older dwarf tugged thoughtfully on a braid of his beard. "Aye, it could be much longer… or not. Later births are swifter, and the new little one might be more impatient than its elder sister."

As if his words were a powerful summons, the door to the house flung open, and the midwife—a matronly dwarvish woman, as there were no human midwives to be found so high on the mountain— bustled out, a beaming smile on her face.

"The waiting's over, my good sir! Your good wife is well…" The woman paused, building up the anticipation, as a sigh of relief left Kiúli, a tense weight washing away from his shoulders. "You now have another daughter to add to your name!"

Kiúli's eyes widened, and a delighted smile spread across his face. "Another daughter?" he looked down at Svanhilda in his lap, who was watching the happenings with wide eyes. "Do you hear that, little one? You have a little sister, now."

"A little sister?" Svanhilda echoed curiously.

"That's a big responsibility, pebble," Grandfather Alvíss said. "Can I trust you're up to the challenge?"

Svanhilda tipped her head to one side. "Re-spons-bilty?"

"It means," Kiúli explained, "that since you're older and wiser, it'll be your job to look after the new baby."

"Oh," Svanhilda pushed out her bottom lip and contemplated this.

"Besides, little rock," Grandfather said, leaning close and

whispering, "having a little sister around can be fun—a playmate all your own!"

"Oh!" That sounded very nice, and Svanhilda lit up. "All right!"

Kiúli shot his father-in-law an appreciative look over his daughter's head, and Alvíss' eyes twinkled merrily back at him.

To Svanhilda's and Althjóf's disappointment, they were forced to wait a half-hour more ere the midwife emerged once again and declared Ingiborg and the new baby were ready to hold court.

Kiúli went first, as was his right, while Alvíss stayed back and kept Svanhilda company. Althjóf kept himself busy, sketching out a design for something with a stick of charcoal on a piece of parchment.

Alvíss had finished two stories and was most of the way through a third when the door opened again, and Kiúli emerged with a beaming smile from the house.

"Hey now, duckling," he said, his enthusiasm shining from him like the rising of the sun. "Do you want to see the new baby?"

Svanhilda nodded eagerly, scrambling and tumbling out of her grandfather's lap, small legs rushing across the clearing and straight into her Papa's arms. Kiúli caught her neatly and swung her up onto his hip, turning to eye his father-in-law with a smile.

"Are you coming, Master Alvíss?"

Grandfather grinned ruefully and waved a hand, shifting his legs under him to stand up. "Yes, yes, I'll come along. But go ahead and don't keep the pebble waiting any longer. I'll come in my own good time."

Kiúli nodded, and with that, he turned and carried Svanhilda into the house.

Ingiborg was reclining on her bed, propped up by pillows, a blanket tucked around her shoulders and her sweat-dampened red hair tied neatly into a braid. Cradled in her arms was a bundle of blankets, clutched close and sweetly to her breast. At Kiúli and Svanhilda's entrance, the lady looked up, and a warm smile crossed her face.

"There you are, child! Come, Svanhilda; come and meet your sister."

Kiúli set his daughter down carefully on the floor, and Svanhilda immediately did as she was bid, and trotted across the room to her mother's side. Obligingly, Ingiborg lowered her bundle so Svanhilda could see better: a small, pink face and squinched shut eyes, a sleepy, open mouth, and abundant, damp strands of reddish hair.

"This is your little sister, Svanhilda. It'll be your job to look after her now," Kiúli said, stroking Svanhilda's hair. Svanhilda nodded, still staring at the baby.

"She's very small," Svanhilda said.

"She's supposed to be that way," Ingiborg said smilingly.

"You were that small, once," Kiúli said, ruffling Svanhilda's hair.

The little girl snapped her head around, eyes wide. "Truly?"

Svanhilda's mother and father burst out laughing, and Svanhilda pouted. She was distracted from her pique, however, when the door opened and Grandfather strode in, his booming, gravel-voice rolling across the floor.

"So, where's the new little pebble?"

Svanhilda waved one hand eagerly towards her grandfather. "Here! Over here! It's the really small person here!"

"Really?" Alvíss replied seriously even as he shared a laughing glance with the adults in the room. "Well, then, I shall have to see this tiny person."

He came and joined them, leaning forward to see the baby better, and grinned. "So this is the little impatient one? She came so much faster than Svanhilda, here. She'll keep you busy, I guarantee it."

As if on cue, the baby began to squirm in her bundle, making tiny, distressed noises at being kept still.

"It's true," Ingiborg laughed. "Svanhilda took her time, but this little one didn't want to wait, I think." She held the baby close to her and rocked her soothingly, breathing gentle assurances against the baby's downy head.

"And she has my hair, it seems," Alvíss said, extremely pleased. "She'll be quite the beauty when she grows up."

"I have no doubt of that," Kiúli said calmly, reaching out and stroking his knuckle along the baby's cheek tenderly. "However, I would count her beauty as an inheritance from her mother's features rather than her grandfather's hair."

Alvíss raised his bushy eyebrows and leaned towards Svanhilda.

"Well, pebble? What do you think?"

Svanhilda pursed her lips thoughtfully, tipping her head to one side as she eyed the baby. "She's pretty!"

"Indeed, she is." Alvíss replied. "And why's that?"

"Uhh…" Svanhilda rubbed her nose, brow furrowed. "'Cause mama's pretty, that's why!"

"Yes, yes she is," Alvíss affirmed as his shoulders slumped dramatically. Kiúli had the grace to not laugh in his face. After a moment, though, the baby's grandfather brushed it off with a twinkle in his eye and turned his attention to the little face of the squirming child. "Well? Have you picked out a name for the little one, yet?"

Kiúli and Ingiborg shared a speaking glance. Kiúli nodded with a smile, and Ingiborg smiled in return and turned her gaze onto her firstborn. "Svanhilda, do you remember how you got your name?"

"Uh-huh!" Svanhilda nodded, but then paused. "…But you can tell it 'gain, if you wanna."

Kiúli was the one who started, sitting down by his wife, and pulling Svanhilda into his lap as Alvíss found a stool. "When you were born, duckling, it was spring. Everything was bright and fresh and new, just as you were. And all over the mountain, the rowan trees were blossoming, as lovely and bright a white as the feathers of a swan. So, your mother and I named you *Svanhilda*, in memory of the swan-white trees that covered the mountain."

Svanhilda nodded, eyes wide.

"So," Ingiborg picked up the thread of the conversation, "we kept that in mind when we knew the new baby was coming. This morning, as I felt the first of the pains, I looked outside at the rowan trees. Since it is autumn, the white blossoms are long gone away; instead, the rowan trees carry crowns of fruit, bright and beautiful as rubies, red as roses. So, we picked out a name thus."

"My beloved, newest daughter—" Kiúli said, his voice full of pride as he carefully laid a hand on the baby's ruddy head, "Rósfrída."

"The beloved, beautiful rose." Alvíss nodded solemnly. "It is a good name."

"Rósfrída," Ingiborg said softly, and the baby let out a mew, stilling for the first time in minutes. "Welcome to the world, Rósfrída my darling."

"Rose-free-da," Svanhilda said slowly, carefully, and then laid her little hand on Rósfrída's stomach solemnly. "Nice to meechu."

Rósfrída let out another little mew, and Ingiborg turned her attention to her eldest daughter. "Svanhilda, as her big sister, it's your job to be Rósfrída's friend and watch out for her. Can you do it?"

Svanhilda nodded earnestly, and Ingiborg smiled. "Good—I'm glad. Here's something I want you to remember, so listen carefully."

The little girl nodded again, and Ingiborg let her gaze drift down towards the baby in her arms again. "You are siblings; there are many precious things in this world, but nothing so precious as the bond between you two. So, promise me, daughter of mine… whatever one of you has, she must share it with her sister. Don't let something so small as a possession tear you apart. And even more importantly than that—you must always stick together. Sisters are strongest when they are together! Do you promise?"

Svanhilda blinked at her mother, and then at the baby, biting her lip. If mama asked for a promise like that, it must be very important, so she nodded. "I p'omise, mama." Then she leaned forward, placing her hand on Rósfrída's stomach again.

"D'you hear, Ros-free-da?" She said in what she believed to be a whisper, and her parents and grandfather graciously pretended they could not hear. "I'mma share everyfing I have wif you, and you'll share everyfing wif me, cause we're sisters and tha's a special, special treasure. And I'll stay by you and make sure you're safe. I p'omise."

Rósfrída blinked open her newborn-blue eyes and stared up into the sky blue of her sister's, and opened her tiny, gummy mouth. Svanhilda decided then and there it wouldn't be a burden to share everything alike with her little sister and stay by her and look after her. She was certain that mama, and papa, and grandfather were right.

The bond between siblings—between *sisters*—was a special treasure indeed.

>>*<< · >>*<< · >>*<<

11

CHAPTER 2

The forest was dim, clinging to the edges of winter, the creeping edges of twilight beginning to clutch and cling to the bare arms of the trees. Thick, heavy clouds slowly marched across the sky, white with the promise of snow.

Amongst the gathering shadows of evening, Tryggvi plodded along slowly, his small form slipping in and out between the shadows of the trees. He was a small boy, with the passage of no more than five or six winters to his name.

The boy's cold fingers clutched tightly to a round amber stone, hanging from a braided leather cord about his neck, his eyes fixed on the path ahead. It was a special necklace… a gift from Tryggvi's mother, for his last birthday.

'It is a powerful stone, from far, far, away—across the sea. An amber eye, which will allow you to see things that others cannot. Promise me you'll never take it off, Tryggvi? If you ever get lost in the woods, it will lead you straight and safely as long as you hold it tight.'

The little boy hastily rubbed his sleeve across his eyes, trying hard not to start crying again. He was very, very tired, and his feet hurt, and he was very cold. He missed Mama... and Papa… and everyone. He missed *home*.

But *home*…

His footsteps stuttered for a moment, but he straightened his little weary shoulders as best he could and stomped on. Mama had made him *promise* not to turn around, not *ever*, and Papa said warriors never break their promises.

So Tryggvi kept on walking, and walking, clutching the amber stone, his shoulders slumping and feet dragging, wondering why his stomach had stopped pinching him a while back.

He only stopped when the first snowflake, fat and white and soft, drifted down lazily from the heavens and landed on the loam beneath his feet.

Tryggvi may have been young, but his Papa and Mama had already been teaching him about the forest that surrounded his home. After all, Mama said, her people were of the forests, so it was only fitting he knew as much as he could about them.

He may have been young, but he knew what happened when little boys were out alone in the woods in a snowstorm at night…

…he would end up with Mama and Papa after all, and Mama and Papa wouldn't like that, not with all they'd done to keep him from not going with them.

So Tryggvi huddled in the best shelter he could find—a little crevice formed by the roots of an ancient oak tree, wrapping his arms about his chest, and burying his nose in the crook of his elbow, as if he could escape the cold by hiding.

"Mama," he whispered into the darkness behind his squeezed-shut eyes, "Mama, you promised the stone would help me find friends. Where are they?"

The air was thick with the silence of snow, the flakes floating down slowly and gently. Tryggvi panted in the cold air, his throat stinging, exhaustion flooding his limbs after his head-long flight. He may be little, but as soon as that first flake began to fall, he knew… he knew that there wasn't much hope.

"I'm sorry, Mama. I tried to run away, Mama, like you said." The tears were warm on his cheeks, and he sniffled. "Sorry I couldn't do it."

At least… he thought, *at least I will be with Mama and Papa again soon.*

But… "But I don't really want to go…" he whispered.

The silence didn't answer, and he bowed under its weight, feeling tiny and powerless and the cold leach the strength from his limbs as he sat there, collapsed at the foot of a tree, all alone in the forest as snow continued to fall.

Something cold and wet and slimy dragged across the back of his neck.

Tryggvi screamed, jerked wildly, and fell over face-first in the snow-spotted dirt. A weight landed on his back and scurried up his spine and onto his head, breathing heavily and sniffing in his ear. Tryggvi shut his eyes and waited for the end to come.

A cold, slimy sensation in his ear was replaced by an equally wet, warm thing dragging repeatedly up and down the shell of it. Tryggvi thought if this was some monster of the forest come to devour him, it surely had a strange way of doing it.

Then he remembered he was a jarl's son, not some lowborn boy with no mettle in his heart. He would not lie here, cowering, waiting for death! He pushed himself upright in a mighty surge to face his opponent—

Only to find himself face-to-face with a tiny silvery-gray fluffball, not much larger than Tryggvi's own head, staring at him with wide black eyes.

Tryggvi blinked.

The fluffball stuck out its tongue and licked his nose.

It seemed he was hasty in believing his end had come; he was pretty sure little puppies didn't eat boys. Tentatively, he reached out and carded his cold-blanched fingers through the puppy's soft, silvery fur. "Hello," he said quietly. After all, Mama had taught him it was important to be polite.

'Hello!' the puppy snuffled happily, butting his nose against Tryggvi's wrist in an attempt to gain more attention, and Tryggvi felt his cracking lips turn up into a smile.

"FRODE! Come on! Where are you?" a voice called out, cutting through the empty silence of the winter-edged woods. "We need to get back, or Mother will be mad!"

The little dog's head jerked up, ears twitching, before it turned to give Tryggvi one last reassuring lick across his cheek. *'I'll be back.'* The next moment it had bounded out of the little hollow, charging in the direction of the voice.

Tryggvi sat there, shivering, feeling his thoughts slowly slogging through the mud of his mind. He needed help, but he knew that sometimes there were bad people who didn't want to offer it.

Besides… he thought, his limbs trembling in the cold, Tryggvi wasn't sure he'd be able to get up if he wanted.

"There you are, Frode! C'mon, we don't wanna be out too late, and the snow's start--Hey! Where are you going, silly?"

There was a bark, the high-pitched snapping of a puppy, but still holding the underlying sharpness and volume he would gain as an adult. In fact, it seemed to be getting louder—or was it closer? Tryggvi realized only just in time for the little gray fluffball to burst back into sight, running as fast as its small legs could carry it, his tongue flapping enthusiastically in the wind. Behind him was a boy, a couple years older than Tryggvi, racing to keep up, cloak flapping in a similar manner to the puppy's tongue. Then his gaze happened to catch on Tryggvi, and he stumbled for a second, eyes wide. The next moment he was running again, even faster, and he skidded to his knees beside the hollow where Tryggvi huddled.

"Good boy, Frode!" the boy gasped out, and the puppy yipped in response, flopping down exhaustedly on its belly, and wagging its tiny fluffy curl of a tail. The boy turned to look at Tryggvi, dark blue eyes darting up and down Tryggvi's huddled form, his head tipped to one side. He grinned and stuck out a hand. "Hello!" he said. "My name's Ásbjörn, but my friends call me Björn. What's yours?"

Tryggvi stared at him, and his cold fingers crept up to clutch at the amber-eye pendant that hung around his neck. Mama said it was a *special* necklace from far away, and it would help him see clearly, and it had led him through the woods before he'd got too tired and cold to move any more. Would it show him if this boy was nice?

He wrapped the pendant in his cold fingers and stared hard and hard at the boy called Ásbjörn. But as hard as he stared, he could only see warmth and kindness.

Relief swamped down on him, and he felt a bright grin cross his face, and he stuck a hand out in turn, proudly clasping Ásbjörn's arm like Papa's warriors did, making him feel rather grown-up indeed.

"I'm Tryggvi. Nice ta meet ya!" he chirped.

Ásbjörn smiled elatedly at the sounding of a name, then tipped his head to one side, long wheaten locks feathering around his shoulders, dark eyes concerned. "Are you alright? Do you need me to help you find your mother or father?"

All at once, the grin disappeared, and Tryggvi drooped, his stubby golden braids hanging past his ears. "No, don't gots them no more.”

“No family at all?” Ásbjörn asked gently, and Tryggvi shook his head, once, hard and sharp.

Ásbjörn frowned, and folded his arms, thinking hard. If Tryggvi didn’t have any family at all, that meant he was all alone—and that wouldn’t do.

“Right!” Ásbjörn said firmly, slapping his palms to his thighs, causing Tryggvi’s head to shoot up curiously. “Since you don’t have any family, I’ll give you mine!”

Tryggvi blinked, silver-grey eyes wide and bewildered. “Eh?”

“I’ll be your big brother,” Ásbjörn said earnestly, “and I promise I’ll be the best one I can!”

Tryggvi blinked again, looking lost. “B-but, you, you’re not my kin—”

Ásbjörn snorted. “Who says? *I* say I am, and that’s all that matters.” He paused, then glanced at the littler boy hopefully, “If you want me, that is?”

Tryggvi bit his lip, and squeezed his pendant tight—but again, all he saw was warmth and kindness… and now a new thing, fresh as a sprout from a new-planted seed but growing in strength already. Something a little like what Mama used to have, but different in a way Tryggvi couldn’t explain.

“I..” He bit his lip, then blurted, “That sounds nice.”

Ásbjörn smiled, fierce and happy. “That settles it!” He stood up, and before Tryggvi could even blink, he’d been hauled onto Björn’s back, his arms slung over the older boy’s shoulders and around his neck, Björn’s hands hoisting his knees at little higher.

“Right!” Ásbjörn said, and he set off at a trot through the woods, Frode scampering along happily at his heels. “Don’t worry about anything, I’ll get us both home soon, where we can make it official, and then get you something to eat. You look like you need it!” His voice was cheerful, cutting through and banishing the snow-laden silence, so that the drifting flakes here and there didn’t feel so lonely any longer. “I can tell you’ll be a bit of trouble, but that’s all right. Father told me that it’s an older brother’s job to worry, so leave it all to me!”

Tryggvi wrinkled his nose at that—that sounded like an awfully large burden for one person—but for now he decided he'd just bask in the bright, warm presence Ásbjörn gave off, and let his head rest comfortably on his older brother's shoulder.

There was a village on the hills beside the deep waters of the fjords, the lights shining warm and welcomingly from the windows.

As soon as the lights came into view, Ásbjörn picked up his pace, the nearness of his destination lending speed to his limbs. Tryggvi, at this point, barely noticed, with his face buried in Björn's shoulder and the heaviness of sleep dragging at his mind. The next thing he knew, Ásbjörn was knocking on a wooden door while Frode barked cheerfully, and the door swung open to reveal golden light and warm, friendly chatter.

"Ásbjörn? What's that you've dragged in?"

"He's my new brother," Ásbjörn said seriously. "And he's very hungry and cold, so I need to take care of him."

The man looked down at Ásbjörn, who stared up at him gravely, and then at the huddled form on Ásbjörn's back, and smiled kindly, reaching out and ruffling the older boy's flaxen locks. "Your mother should be waiting for you in her chambers."

Ásbjörn lit up, and carefully hefted up Tryggvi from where he had slipped down and set off through the hall. Tryggvi sunk even deeper into his stupor, reveling in the warmth and comfort this new place gave.

Finally, Ásbjörn came to a stop and knocked once more, and a woman's voice, kind and warm, summoned him in.

"Is that you, my son? You were out longer than you said. I was beginning to grow worried. Did you have a good hunt?"

"The best!" Ásbjörn said. "I found a new brother!"

"A new brother?" the woman asked gently, leaning over Ásbjörn and gently touching Tryggvi's head, fingers carding softly through his golden hair. "Did this new brother of yours agree with his new status?"

"M-hm!" the boy replied, nodding firmly. "He said he didn't have anyone, so I offered to be someone for him." He took a deep breath, before finally admitting, "Also, father said you were sad because you weren't able to give me a little brother, so I found one of my own— so you don't need to be sad anymore."

His mother smiled softly, her eyes a strange melding of sad and happy, and she leaned forward and kissed Ásbjörn gently on the forehead. "That is kind of you indeed. Since the boy has no family of his own, I will be glad beyond measure to welcome him into ours. Set him down and run and tell your father what has happened."

Tryggvi felt kind hands carefully assist Ásbjörn, lifting his body off his brother's back and laying it to rest on something warm and soft. A blanket was drawn over him, and Frode wriggled up to his side, laying down and snuffling his snout into a nook between Tryggvi's arm and the pallet.

"Sleep now, child," the woman said, smoothing her hand over Tryggvi's forehead. "We will be here when you wake."

And with those words, the last of Tryggvi's fears were wiped away, and he let himself set sail on the sea of dreams.

When Tryggvi stirred awake, it was to the feeling of something being poked, repeatedly, against his nose. His nose twitched and wrinkled, then he let out a resounding sneeze.

"Mother, Tryggvi's awake!" a familiar voice yelled from nearby, and Tryggvi jumped.

Another voice floated back—a woman's, calm and refined. "He had better have woken on his own, my son, or I will be displeased indeed."

There was a sound of awkward shuffling, and Tryggvi blinked his eyes blearily to see his new older brother crouched down by his pallet, a guilty look on his face and a long piece of straw grasped in his hand.

Tryggvi blinked sleepily at it.

His nose itched.

His brother shot him a hopeful look. "You woke up on your

own—right, little brother?"

Tryggvi stared at the straw and rubbed his nose.

Ásbjörn dropped it.

"Well?" the woman said, appearing in Tryggvi's field of vision. She was dressed finely, like Mama did, and had long pale hair twined in a thick braid. She took a seat at the foot of Tryggvi's pallet, alighting as gracefully as a bird upon a twig. Her eyes, sharp and blue as ice, swept over the two boys, seeing everything. "Did Ásbjörn wake you up, Tryggvi?"

Tryggvi shot Ásbjörn a look and sneezed. It was all the woman needed to see, for she sighed and shook her head. "Ásbjörn, didn't I tell you Tryggvi needs his rest? You should have left him to sleep. He would have woken when he was ready to."

Ásbjörn frowned, dragging his toes along a seam in the floorboards. "...I just wanted to make sure he was all right."

The woman's stern expression melted, ice transforming into the soft and gentle blue of the morning sky, and she reached out and cradled Ásbjörn's cheek gently. "I understand, my son, but you should listen to me. There's a reason little boys are given mothers."

Tryggvi flinched at that and gripped the blankets covering his lap with his fingers, feeling dampness welling up behind his eyes. The woman—Ásbjörn's mother—must have been observant, for she noticed immediately, and spun to face Tryggvi.

"Oh, I am sorry, little one," she said gently, and wrapped her arms around Tryggvi and cradled him gently to her breast. "The wound is still bleeding for you, is it not?"

Tryggvi relaxed into her hold. It was warm and soft, smelling faintly of smoke from the cook fires, and a little like flowers and soap. She smelled an awful lot like his Mama, but maybe that was just the way mamas were supposed to smell. It made him want to cry a little more, but it also made him want to cry less, so he decided to stop trying to figure out what he was feeling and simply relaxed in a hold that made him feel safe.

"My son tells me that you have no family… is that true?" Her voice was gentle and low, soothing as a lullaby. "You need not tell me, if you wish not."

The boy bit his lip, sallying his courage, and nodded, his voice quiet and subdued. "It's true."

"I am sorry," the lady said. "I know there is nothing I can do to undo your loss, child, however… my son tells me that he has made you his brother?"

Tryggvi nodded. "Uh-huh."

"Well, then," she said, her voice gentle, "if you are Ásbjörn's brother, and Ásbjörn is my son, would that not make you my son as well?"

Tryggvi sniffled a bit as he thought that over, and the lady waited patiently, lifting a piece of cloth and helping him blow his nose. Finally, he nodded and said, "I suppose that makes sense."

"I'm glad," Ásbjörn's mother said, and smiled kindly, wrapping her arms around Tryggvi again and pressing a kiss to his brow. "I promise I will care for you as I do Ásbjörn, and may you never suffer want for love or anything else."

Tryggvi flushed and tugged nervously at one of his braids, and asked quietly, "Do I have to call you Mama now?"

"You can call me whatever you want," the lady said decisively, "and in your own time. If you never wish to call me 'Mama', then don't."

The little boy nodded, and a feeling of cool relief swept through his chest. He could barely think the word 'mama' without an image of his own mother flashing before his eyes. That was a wound too fresh to touch. "What shall I call you then?"

"Well," she said thoughtfully, "you are my son's brother, and my child, so it would be best and most fitting if you refer to me as kin. You may call me Aunt Ljúfvina if you wish."

Tryggvi nodded, feeling exhaustion sweep over him again, and spoke through a yawn, "That'd be nice."

"Is he falling asleep again?" He heard Ásbjörn pipe up, disappointment in his voice. "But he just woke up."

"I imagine Tryggvi's had a few very tiring days. He needs his rest," Ljúfvina said gently. "Don't worry. He will wake when he is ready, and the two of you will be able to run about to your heart's content. But for now he must sleep, and for now *you* must leave him to it."

"Yes, mother," Ásbjörn said sadly. "What are you going to do?"

"Me?" Ljúfvina laughed. "I'm going to inform my lord husband of our new son."

When Tryggvi woke again, the room was empty, but he could hear the sounds of merriment and feasting nearby. His stomach rumbled, so he scooted to the edge of his pallet and tiptoed across the floor barefoot. He had just reached the corner when a shadow darkened the path before him, and a tall lady stepped into view. Tryggvi took a careful step backwards, nerves climbing their way into his stomach as little fingers reached for the pendant hanging from his neck.

She seemed vaguely familiar, but then she smiled and Tryggvi's heart filled with relief and warmth. He knew this lady. "Aunt Ljúfvina!"

Her smile brightened and her eyes lit up, and she knelt gracefully before him, clapping her hands together. "So, you do remember me! I'm very glad to see you up and about, Tryggvi, child. Do you have need of anything?"

Cheeks flushing, he shook his head adamantly, but his stomach decided at that moment to cut all ties of loyalty to Tryggvi and rumbled loudly. His cheeks immediately turned redder, but Ljúfvina didn't laugh. Instead, she simply smiled and held out a hand. "Would you like to come and get something to eat? The hall is having dinner, now."

Tryggvi still couldn't quite muster up the nerve to speak, but he reached out shyly and took her hand. With that, she led him into the feasting hall.

The hall was a glorious contrast of bright firelight and deep, flickering shadows, darting across the beams of the room in a mysterious dance, swaying in time to the movements of the people seated on the benches below.

Their entrance went unnoticed at first—but then a little boy who sat at the High Table spotted them, and he immediately scrambled out of his seat and ran across the floor to where Ljúfvina and Tryggvi stood, a bright smile shining on his face and an eager puppy flopping along at his heels. "You're finally awake!"

Tryggvi nodded shyly, the words still seeming lost to him. Ásbjörn's smile shone even brighter, and he flung his arms around the younger boy, wrapping him in a tight bear hug, lifting the smaller boy clear into the air. "I'm so glad you're feeling better! I've been worried about you." Meanwhile, Frode sniffed happily around Tryggvi's dangling ankles, letting out small yips here and there. *New person sleeps no more! Hurray!'*

The younger boy felt that warm spot in his belly grow and begin to spread, flooding his limbs with warmth. Hesitantly, his arms reached out and hugged Ásbjörn back, which seemed to prompt Ásbjörn—his big brother now—to squeeze him all the tighter. When Ásbjörn stepped back, Tryggvi felt a rush of cold air, and wished he could stay wrapped up in that embrace a while longer.

It reminded him of … of back home, of family, just like Aunt Ljúfvina's hug had. He had felt so lonely and cold for so long, that now he felt he couldn't get enough of that warmth—and yet he couldn't quite bring himself to reach out for it. So, he was stuck there, in that limbo of lonely yearning, hovering on the edge of the firelight and yet not quite daring to step into the circle of warmth of his own accord.

However, Ásbjörn was not a fire, for fires had not hands with which to reach out and help.

Tryggvi felt his hand grabbed by Ásbjörn, who tugged him gently towards one end of the room. Frode eagerly scampered circles around about them and Ljúfvina glided behind, as graceful as a swan. No one marked their passage, absorbed in their feast and merriment, for the snow had fallen thickly on the fjord and had put a stop to all work without. But this could not bring down the Folkbiörn, the people of that kingdom. According to their custom, they fought back against the dark and cold of the depth of winter with firelight and laughter and good food and ale, for they were a fighting people, and would not be defeated by winter so easily. So it was that their passing by was unnoticed, which Tryggvi greatly preferred, and they reached the High Table at the back wall at last.

There was a great chair of pale white beach wood, carved all over with strange and wondrous forms—most noticeably that of a great bear—which could be seen on the arms and on the back of the chair. In that chair sat a great man, tall and broad-shouldered, with hair orange as a sunset and a long beard as forked as a serpent's tongue. He was as big as a great bear, and Tryggvi felt very small next to him, standing at the foot of his grand chair—as small as Frode, who had been distracted by fallen scraps nearby.

Ásbjörn squeezed his hand then, strong and sure, and Aunt Ljúfvina set her warm hand on his shoulder, a gentle, steadying warmth, and Tryggvi mustered the courage to look up at the man before him. It was a good thing he did, for it was only then he noticed that the gigantic, intimidating man had Ásbjörn's eyes—dark blue as the night sky, filled with kindness that shone like stars.

Suddenly, Tryggvi didn't feel tiny and weak at all—or if he did, it was in a good way, for there was nothing to fear in being small next to this man. His back was wide and strong enough to keep Tryggvi and Björn and Frode and Aunt Ljúfvina all safe, and he had a heart that would protect them without hesitation.

The man slipped from his great chair to kneel on the ground before Ásbjörn and Tryggvi, and he smiled.

"Well, my son has informed me he has found himself a new brother. Is that true, young one?"

Tryggvi nodded firmly. "Yes, sir! I'm Tryggvi."

The man's smile grew wider, and he held out a hand. "Well met, then, young Tryggvi. I am Ólaf, Ásbjörn's father and King of these lands, and you may call me Uncle if you wish, or whatever name seems best to you."

Tryggvi blinked, then smiled. "Oh, Papa used to talk about King Ólaf. He said you were a good man." In the light of this discovery, he forgot everything, reveling in the familiarity that banished for a moment his uncertainty and sorrow.

"Oh?" The King blinked. "And… if you do not mind answering, young one, who was your father?"

Now that was a hard question indeed, for Tryggvi didn't use Papa's name very much, but if he thought hard enough about it, he remembered what mama and the jarls would call him. "Papa's name is Éldi!"

Ólaf's bush-like brows shot up his forehead, and then his eyes grew sad. Ásbjörn looked confused, but Ljúfvina's grip tightened on Tryggvi's shoulder in surprise and consternation. "King Éldi Fullspakr?"

Tryggvi remembered that when people he didn't know came and spoke to Papa, they would call him *Fullspakr,* so he nodded firmly. "Uh-huh."

"I see," Ólaf said heavily, his eyes downcast. "It seems that even ill news travels slowly in winter." He paused and set his hand on Tryggvi's free shoulder. "Do you have no home to go to?"

The boy had forgotten, for a moment, that Papa was gone, but he remembered now, and the sadness came back. Tryggvi swallowed hard and shook his head once. "…No. Everyone's gone. Papa, and Mama… and everyone."

"Well, then… if you have no home to go to, then I shall simply have to share mine." Tryggvi blinked past his sadness up at Ásbjörn's father, who smiled down at the small boy. "Would you like to be picked up?"

Tryggvi glanced at Ásbjörn, who grinned and nodded, and then nodded to the man. Ólaf grinned, and in one smooth, practiced move, swept the boy up onto his shoulder and rose into the air, turning to the crowd of feasters.

"HO, THERE, PEOPLE OF MY HALL!" he bellowed, his voice deep and loud as a horn. Instantly, silence drenched the hall, and the attention of everyone in the hall was riveted on the man at the head of the table, and the boy perched on his shoulder.

"My son Ásbjörn found a child these three days past, lost in the wood on the edge of a storm, and brought him home and called him brother. Here now, before all of you as witness, I acknowledge by son's decision, and I name Tryggvi here my son, of my blood and of my heirs, as long as the roots of the mountains still stand firm and as long as the waves crash on the shore, and longer still! So welcome him, and count him among our people, for now and always! Hail and well met!"

"Hail and well met!" The people in the hall yelled out as one, with such a force of warmth and welcome that Tryggvi thought it nearly enough to knock all his loneliness away. Ólaf picked Tryggvi off his shoulder and sat down, setting the boy on his knee instead. The next moment Ásbjörn had scrambled up on his father's other knee, grinning brightly, and Queen Ljúfvina drew close, taking a seat upon the arm of the chair and setting a hand on her husband's shoulder. Tryggvi grinned back at Ásbjörn, feeling warm and full and safe.

Ólaf gripped the shoulders of the two boys and beamed proudly. "Well, now, the Lea of Flame in the Highest Heaven must have sent the Wanderer to give me a great gift—for now I have not one, but two fine sons! My fortune is blessed indeed!"

"Welcome to our hall, my son," Ljúfvina said warmly, and smoothed her fingers over Tryggvi's rumpled locks.

The moment she was done, Ásbjörn flung an arm over Tryggvi's shoulder and knocked their heads together gently. "Welcome home, little brother! I'll look after you now and always, I promise."

And Tryggvi wrapped himself around the warm feeling in his heart—new and different, and very little like what had once been his… but it still meant *home*, all the same.

CHAPTER 3

The smell of supper, a mix of meat and bread and woody smoke curling in the air, was wafting through the house. Mama was standing by the fire, tending to supper, while Svanhilda was distracting Rósfrída—or trying to, anyway. Rósfrída was not easily distracted.

Ever since the littler of the sisters had learned to walk, she had begun to walk *everywhere*—and what was worse, she had begun to climb. She had only just passed her third winter, but she was spending nearly all her time climbing up every tree and rock that could be found—that is, when she was not running hither and thither over the grass like a baby rabbit. When she was inside and away from trees and rocks, she scaled the walls instead and clung to the rafters.

Svanhilda didn't know how she was supposed to watch over a little sister like that, because Svanhilda wouldn't be caught more than her own head's height above the ground, unless it be from Papa's shoulders. Her feet were made for the ground, after all; she had stone in her bones and iron in her blood, as Grandfather would say. Svanhilda was a child of the mountain.

But Rósfrída… Rósfrída was a creature of the wind and sea, just like Papa. And neither the wind nor the sea like staying still, and they cannot be contained.

With a sigh, Svanhilda eyed her little sister, who was currently standing on some piece of furniture, poised on her tiptoes and arms straining for her next handhold, tongue poking out of her mouth in concentration.

With another sigh and a shake of her head, Svanhilda propped her fists on her hips and lifted her chin. "Rósfrída, where are you going?"

"High."

Svanhilda frowned. "Mama says we're s'posed to stick together, right?"

Rósfrída paused, drawing her hand back from reaching out for her next handhold, turning her head to look at her elder sister. "Uh-huh!"

"I can't stick with you if you're up there! Don't go somewhere I can't follow."

"Oh." Rósfrída looked around, tucking several knuckles into her mouth and sucking on them musingly. "Svana come wif me?"

Svanhilda huffed and shook her head firmly, braids smacking against her shoulders. "I can't! I don't like being high like that."

"But high's *fun*," Rósfrída pointed out confusedly. "Come see!"

"*No*," her big sister said, even more firmly. "I really don't like it! You'll have to come down."

Rósfrída face turned very sad. "A-righ', Svana." She gripped her handholds and shifted in preparation to climb down, before pausing.

"…Svana?"

"Yes?"

Rósfrída's bottom lip stuck out in a pout. "Stuck."

Svanhilda sighed, shaking her head, before skipping a couple steps away to call out to Mama. "Mama, Rósfrída is stuck up in the rafters again."

Mama looked up from her cooking, glanced over, and sighed. But the sigh drew a smile from the corners of her mouth, and she shook her head fondly before stepping to the door of the house. "Kiúli, Rósfrída is in need of help."

"Oh no, dare I guess?" Kiúli said cheerfully and stood up from where he was carving outside the door, brushing the wood shavings from his knees before he stepped inside. "Where is my little wanderer this time?"

"Papa! Help!" Rósfrída called, lifting one hand in a wave that caused Svanhilda's heart to clench and Ingiborg to frown nervously. Kiúli merely smiled and strode over, crossing his arms and eyeing the situation.

"You climbing again, little flower?"

"Uh-huh!" Rósfrída said eagerly. "Wanna get high, but Svana says *no* so I *tries* to get down but now I's stuck."

"Hmm. I see." Her father responded, crouching down to get a better view. "You know, sweetling, if you want to keep climbing, you're going to have to know how to get yourself out of a sticky place. I might not be able to help you right away. You got up there, sweetling, so you can get down again. I believe in you; you can do this."

Rósfrída pouted and shook her head, clinging all the more firmly to the wall. "No! I can't, I'mma stuck. Don't know how to get down!"

Kiúli smiled gently. "That's all right. I'm here now, aren't I? I'll help you figure it out, and if you mess up, I'll catch you. Are you ready?"

Rósfrída was still pouting, but after several moments, she gave a nod. And so, slowly, carefully, Kiúli coached the little girl down the wall and safely onto the floor. The instant her feet touched solid ground, Rósfrída ran forward and wrapped her arms around her father's legs, squeezing as tight as she could and beaming gratefully up at Kiúli. "Papa! Papa, looksit—I did it!"

Her father laughed and reached down, swinging her up to cradle her securely against his chest. "So you did! Brave and clever girl that you are, I had no doubt of it. Good job, sweetling."

The little girl flung her arms around her father's neck and squeezed as tightly as she could, though it was undoubtedly far less tight than she thought. "Thank you, Papa!"

"Always, sweetling," he said, with a rumbling chuckle. "I'll always do my best to help you when you're stuck."

With a well-practiced movement, Kiúli shifted his youngest so she was cradled securely in only one of his arms, then bent down and scooped up his elder daughter with his free one. Svanhilda giggled; heights were not her favorite, but Papa was safe, so it was all right. Then all three made their way back to the cookfire, where Mama was watching with a fond smile on her face.

Kiúli plopped down and set his girls upon his lap, then smiled up at his wife. "Prepare for company, love, I saw your father coming up the path."

A bright smile crossed Ingiborg's face, but before she could even respond, the door swung open and Alvíss strode inside as if he had been summoned by the mention of his name.

"Grandfather!" the girls squealed and tumbled off of Kiúli's lap to run to meet him.

"My pebbles!" Alvíss laughed and opened his arms to receive them joyfully. "And how are you today!"

"I gots stuck onna wall but Papa helped me, yup!" Rósfrída explained.

"Oh, is that so?" Alvíss nodded solemnly, but he exchanged amused glances with his daughter and her husband. "You're very like your Uncle Nefir; he was always climbing up things as well, though of course your mother wouldn't remember."

"Why's dat?" Rósfrída asked, ever curious.

"Brother Nefir is older than me, of course," Ingiborg said, looking up from her stewpot. "I would have been far too little to remember any climbing escapades, if I was even born at all."

Both Svanhilda and Rósfrída blinked in surprise at this information. "You were little, mama?" Svanhilda asked skeptically.

"Everyone was little once," Kiúli said with a laugh, crouching down beside his two girls and ruffling their hair. "As little as you, and littler."

"Even you, papa?" Rósfrída gasped.

"Even me," Papa said solemnly.

"Even *Grandfather?*" Svanhilda pressed, even more skeptically. Grandfather was *old*, after all. Old as mountains!

"Yes, even me! A long time ago, to be sure, but both your Uncle Althjóf and I were small once." The words began with a hearty laugh, but the cheer steadily leached out of Alvíss' voice by the end of the sentence. Ingiborg and Kiúli shared a look at this; then Ingiborg turned to the girls, smiling gently.

"Daughters, I think the cat must be bored. Why don't you go play with it?"

Rósfrída let out a squeal of excitement at being given permission to bother the cat. Normally, Ingiborg warned her away from the kitty, as Rósfrída tended towards smothering it with her bounding affection, and cats rarely appreciate a child's brand of affection or smothering.

Svanhilda, who was also fond of the cat but old enough to realize it in turn wasn't fond of hugging, dutifully trotted after her sister in her hunt for the cat. Still, bits and pieces of the grown-up's conversation crossed her attention as she did so.

"And how has Uncle Althjóf been?" Ingiborg asked casually, not looking up from where she was tending the pot.

Alvíss huffed out a sigh, shaking his head. "He's in a bit of a snit, right now. Thinks we're not getting paid enough."

"Really?" Kiúli said incredulously. "You're being paid more than I could make in ten years."

The old dwarf shrugged. "We were tasked to simply create a secure vault for the treasures of King Ólaf's family. We *may* have gotten a bit carried away with the design, perhaps…"

Ingiborg smiled, letting out a good-natured, knowing chuckle. "Somehow, I'm not surprised, knowing you, Father."

Alvíss shook his head in a mock-scolding fashion. "Go on, daughter, laugh at your old father." The mirth drained out of his features, however, and he sighed again. "That's what your uncle says people will do, anyway."

Ingiborg looked up from her pot then, a frown creasing her forehead, and Kiúli frowned. "And why is that?"

"The King has showed us what we will be safe-guarding in our vault, and my little brother thinks that since our work is to be the keeper of such vast treasure, we deserve more in return and are fools if we do not demand greater payment." He thew his hands up in the air, growing more exasperated by the moment. "If we were hired to create a beautiful necklace and offered a rich reward for doing so, and at the end we were given a priceless jewel to set in it, would we then demand even more gold simply because the jewel is worth so much? Nay!"

Alvíss scoffed and shook his head. "Does he not understand that the true joy of a dwarf is in the making and crafting of wondrous things? Gold comes in second to such a reward. In the making of such a work, we have been compensated well indeed. Clearly, however, he doesn't think so, and has said he's wasting his skills and talents by working with such a fool as me."

Ingiborg and Kiúli exchanged looks, and Ingiborg sighed, stepping away from the pot and sitting down beside her father, reaching to take his hand. "Don't worry about it too much, father. I'm sure Uncle Althjóf will listen to reason, just given some time."

Her father let out one last, heavy sigh, and shook his head, a smile crossing his face as he reached out to pat her head. "I'm sure you are right, daughter. But he is my little brother, and I cannot help but worry. If he persists in insisting he needs naught but gold to fulfill his life, he'll find his life empty and cold ere long."

"If that is so, then that is his choice," Kiúli said solemnly. "All you can do is offer him what wisdom you have to give."

"You seem experienced with such a thing," Grandfather asked.

Kiúli huffed in amusement. "You meet many a fool on the sea."

"Then the sea is not so different than the mountains," Alvíss retorted with a wry smile. "Save in your boats their heads are full of seawater, and in the mountains they are full of rocks."

Kiúli threw back his head and laughed, and the tension diffused, like thick clouds of smoke swept away by a fresh wind from the sea.

"Speaking of seas and mountains and the difference," Alvíss said, turning back to his daughter, who had risen again to tend dinner, "how have you been?"

Ingiborg smiled. "You know very well how I've been, as you visited me not three weeks ago. But you may tell my band of worrywart siblings that I am doing *just* fine."

"Well, then," Alvíss said, a smile growing on his face, "perhaps you'd be interested in the bag of beads I've set outside the door—"

His daughter's face lit up with a brilliant smile, and Kiúli grinned at her. "Well, I for one am interested—I always fetch the best prices for the bracelets and necklaces you make."

Ingiborg laughed and blushed, and turned her smile back to her father. "Thank you, father. My hands have been itching to handle gold and gems again."

"I thought as much," Alvíss said smugly. "You can take the dwarf-maiden out of the forge, but not the forge out of the dwarf-maiden."

"True," she said with a smile. "But I am mother's daughter, too. I have enough man's blood in me to love the wide sky and the sea wind. You don't have to worry for me, father." She glanced over at Kiúli, and the gaze she shared with her husband was as warm as an afternoon in summer. "I am *quite* happy."

"I'll always worry," her father grumbled. "It's my job. But I can tell you're flourishing here, so I won't kick up too much of a fuss."

"Thank you, Father," Ingiborg said gently, and the conversation turned to other matters.

Once the meal was over, Alvíss arose and said his goodbyes, kissing his daughter and granddaughters before heading off to his home, singing a song of forging as he strode off down the road into the evening's dimness.

Svanhilda sat on her Papa's shoulders, and Rósfrída was cradled in her mother's arms as they waved goodbye until they could see their grandfather no longer. Then they were taken inside and put to bed, and their parents left the two girls to fall asleep while they tended to grown-up matters.

Svanhilda slipped deeper beneath the blankets, and Rósfrída huddled against her side, little fingers reaching out and tugging at the side of Svanhilda's nightgown. "Svana, Svana, why Granfaffer sad?"

"'Cause Grandfather loves Uncle Althjóf a lot, but Uncle Althjóf doesn't want to spend time with him, or something." Svanhilda did her best to explain, even though she didn't really understand herself.

"Silly Uncle," Rósfrída said sadly, her fist tugging again on Svanhilda's nightgown. "Siblins' s'posed to stick together."

Svanhilda hugged Rósfrída tighter, snuggling deeper under the thick warm shield of the coverlet. "That's right," she said firmly. "Brothers and sisters are best and strongest together." A thought struck her, and she scooted back a little, before clumsily clasping Rósfrída's forearm and guiding Rósfrída to do the same to Svanhilda's own. It was a clasp of promise that Papa had taught her. She squeezed her little sister's arm gently and said solemnly, "I, Svanhilda Ingiborgardottir promise this! *We* will not leave each other."

Rósfrída squeezed back and lisped firmly, "Never, never!"

Svanhilda nodded. That dealt with, she shuffled into a more

comfortable position and let herself drift off into sleep. Rósfrída curled into Svanhilda's side and beat her older sister in their journey to the land of dreams.

CHAPTER 4

Tryggvi ran forward, slammed the butt of his faithful stick down into the middle of the creek, and vaulted over the gap with a gleeful shout, swinging gracefully through the air.

His landing was a little less graceful, as his left foot caught beneath a root, and he began to pitch towards the ground.

Luckily, his brother was there.

Ásbjörn caught the back of Tryggvi's tunic and hauled him upright before the younger boy could faceplant in the loam. "You alright there?" he asked with a laugh.

"Yup!" Tryggvi said with a grin, not bothered by the fact he had nearly fallen on his face. "Thanks, Ásbjörn!"

"No problem," his brother replied with a smirk, and hooked his elbow around Tryggvi's neck, hauling the younger boy into his side and aggressively roughing up Tryggvi's hair. "What are big brothers for, 'cept for keeping their troublesome little brothers out of worse trouble?"

Tryggvi squirmed wildly, but Ásbjörn had four years and quite a few inches on the younger boy, so his efforts were futile. "Leg'go! 'M not troublesome!"

His brother snorted. "You're the definition of troublesome."

"Am not!"

"Are too."

"Am not!"

"Are too."

"*Am not!*"

This final 'am not' was accompanied by a swift and vicious movement of Tryggvi's knee directly into the back of Ásbjörn's. This proved sufficient to cross the gap of four years and a great number of inches, as Ásbjörn's leg buckled and his grip loosened enough for Tryggvi to wiggle out to freedom. He promptly used this freedom to tackle Ásbjörn's already unstable legs, sending them both crashing to the forest floor. The noise and violence startled the dog, stirring Frode up into a flurry, darting back and forth and blasting their ears with frenzied barking.

It was some time before the war was over, with Ásbjörn emerging once again as the victor. At the end, however, the two brothers laid side by side, laughing and kicking each other's ankles, Frode running cirlces around them, still merrily barking up a storm.

After a while, Ásbjörn's laughter finally faded into a long, contented sigh, followed by silence. "Wait, what were we doing again?"

Tryggvi immediately popped up, tugging eagerly on Ásbjörn's sleeve. "We're on the hunt for Old King Býulfr's palace! C'mon, let's go!"

"Oh, right," Ásbjörn said, and laughed at Tryggvi's eagerness. "C'mon, let's get going." He jumped to his feet and took Tryggvi's hand, pulling his little brother up too. Tryggvi gathered up his stick and Ásbjörn readjusted his belt, which had been knocked askew in their fight, and the three of them—two boys and their dog—set off into the woods.

"Have you seen it before?" Tryggvi asked curiously, half-skipping every couple steps or so in order to keep up with Ásbjörn's longer legs. Ásbjörn was twelve winters old, and his legs were beginning to stretch as his head began to shoot up towards the treetops, while Tryggvi was only eight, and currently only the appropriate size to act as an elbow-rest for his elder brother.

Mother said that he would doubtlessly grow tall himself and he just had to wait, but waiting wasn't very fun. Tryggvi wanted to be tall *now*.

"Nope," Ásbjörn said, shaking his head as he scanned the forest ahead of him. "But my grandfather did when he was a bit older than us. If Grandfather could find it, I'm sure we can!"

Tryggvi cheered at this and ran forward a few feet with Froda eagerly at his heels, pulling ahead of his brother, if only briefly.

The night before at dinner, the skald had recited the tale of old King Býulfr, who had once lived in a magical palace and could turn into a polar bear during the day, ere he was rescued from a cruel fate by the lady that would one day be his queen. It was a favorite story that Tryggvi had heard many times since he first came to this land, and one which both boys liked, but last night King Ólaf had shared a detail neither of his sons had heard before: that apparently King Ólaf's own father had seen the legendary palace once while wandering through the nearby woods as a boy.

Well. Such a story told to twelve- and eight-year-old boys is as good as an invitation to go adventuring, and so here they were the next day, with their walking sticks, 'provisions', and their dog—the three golden necessities of any good adventure.

"Where are we gonna look first?" he called back, his head swiveling to either side, searching for clues. He supposed he could always ask the trees for directions, but that would be cheating. After all, if Father's father had found it without asking trees for help, then so could they!

"I think Grandfather said it lies to the north of our village," Ásbjörn said. "so, let's search there."

"Right!" Tryggvi said, and turned to the proper direction, nearly hopping in his excitement. "C'mon, Frode! Let's go!" With that, he broke into a run, Frode bounding at his heels, tongue flapping with excitement.

Ásbjörn laughed and broke into a jog, which, with his longer legs, was enough to keep up with his brother.

They ran for a long, long time—or as some might count it, ten minutes—when Tryggvi's side began to ache enough that he stopped. He plopped down at the base of a tree, and Frode flopped down on his belly next to him, panting cheerfully, legs spread out to let the coolness of the loam chill his overheated body. Ásbjörn sat down on a nearby log, somewhat more dignified, and began digging through his pouch in search of a snack. He found some venison jerky; he passed one piece over to Tryggvi, tossed another to the dog who snapped it down, and kept one for himself. Tryggvi took a big bite and chewed enthusiastically.

Once the jerky was demolished, and Ásbjörn had handed over the waterskin for his brother to refresh himself, Tryggvi hopped up onto the log and stood on his tiptoes, shading his eyes as he stared out toward the north. Frode hopped up behind him, sniffing intently.

"How far away is the palace, do you think, big brother?"

Ásbjörn stood up next to him, gazing thoughtfully through the wood. "It can't be *too* far. After all, Alvíss' mountain is to the north, so it must be somewhere between there and here."

Tryggvi stuck out his tongue. Ásbjörn rolled his eyes and smacked the back of his brother's head, grinning at Frode's unhappy bark at the display of violence. "Be respectful, sprat. Alvíss is Father's honored friend!"

Tryggvi huffed furiously. "But he's taking you away!"

"Only for a year and a day, to *study*," Ásbjörn replied. "He'll be teaching me all sorts of things about the world! I'm looking forward to it. It's important things I should know, anyway, since I'll be king."

Tryggvi kicked at the log. His brother grinned and hopped off it, hooking an arm around Tryggvi's neck and dragging him off the log and into his side. "Don't worry, little brother. I'll miss you too. I'll have fun while I'm gone, and you'll have fun here with Mother and Father and Frode and everybody, and I'll be back before you know it! And when you're thirteen, it'll be your turn to go study, and it'll be *my* turn to miss *you*."

Tryggvi opened his mouth to respond, only to pause, and spin to one side. At the same moment, Frode stiffened, his sniffs increasing in intensity. Tryggvi frowned, leaning forward curiously. "Did you hear that?"

Ásbjörn's hand strayed to his knife, his eyes narrowing. "No. What is it?"

"Dunno," Tryggvi said. "But it thinks it's very dangerous."

Ásbjörn raised an eyebrow. "It *thinks* it's dangerous?"

"Uh-huh," Tryggvi said, slightly distracted. He took a couple steps forward curiously, Frode following at his heels. His forward momentum was halted when Ásbjörn snatched the back of his cloak.

"Hold on now, Tryggvi. Neither of us is getting any closer until we know what it is," he said sternly, and Tryggvi pouted in the way of someone who knows the other is right but doesn't want to admit it.

Frode edged to the front and took up a guard position in front of his boys, head lowered, legs braced, and hackles rising skyward. Ásbjörn's hand tightened on his knife. Tryggvi merely fidgeted excitedly.

Both stood there, holding their breaths, listening to the ominous rustle of the leaves as the threat stepped out from behind the tree.

The threat was a kitten.

Both boys relaxed, though Ásbjörn didn't let his hand stray from his knife. Frode's head popped up, however, his tongue lolling out and his tail beginning to pick up speed.

The kitten was very small, clumsily picking its way through the fallen leaves at the base of the tree, a tiny ball of fluff and superiority.

Tryggvi managed to squirm free from his brother's now rather lax grip and crouched down in front of the kitten, holding out his fingers to be sniffed. "Hello there! How'd you get here?"

The kitten deigned to find his fingers as an acceptable offering and sniffed them before rubbing his small chin against the side. *'I was on an adventure, and I smelled something familiar, and I found you instead'.*

"Oh, I'm sorry I wasn't helpful, then!" Tryggvi replied sincerely and scratched gently underneath the kitten's chin. Frode pushed forward eagerly, trying to sniff at the new little friend, but the kitten sent the dog a disdainful glare.

Suitably chastened, Frode tactfully retreated behind Ásbjörn for protection.

"What is that?" Ásbjörn asked, peering curiously over Tryggvi's shoulder. "Is that a cat? Why are you talking to it?"

The tiny ball of fluff bristled in what Tryggvi believed was an attempt to seem intimidating. *'And what is that? A moron? Why are you spending time with it?'*

Tryggvi frowned down at the kitten. "That's not nice. He's my brother; be nice to him."

The kitten sniffed haughtily. *'I am a cat. I am not "nice".'*

Tryggvi laughed. Ásbjörn crouched down beside him, resting his arms on his knees. "I didn't know you could speak to animals."

Tryggvi blinked in surprise. "I haven't told you? But I talk to them all the time."

"You do?"

"Uh-huh. Guess you just didn't notice."

Ásbjörn shook his head, laughing, and ruffled his hair. "I always knew you were special, little brother, but this proves you're even more special than I thought."

The younger grinned cheerfully at the compliment, enduring the assault for several seconds before ducking away, giggling.

The kitten did not appreciate the lack of attention to its most glorious person and sank tiny pinprick claws into Tryggvi's thigh.

It did not hurt very badly, but it hurt enough, with enough force and surprise behind it that Tryggvi let out a yelp.

"I think it wants attention," Ásbjörn said, amused, and Tryggvi stuck out his tongue. But he turned back to the kitten.

It was not particularly large, but big enough that Tryggvi would need both hands to cradle it. Its fur was long and fluffy, a bright golden color, with wide eyes the color of the first leaves in spring. It was a rather handsome young fellow, a fact of which it was clearly aware from the sheer pride evident in every inch of its rather small body.

"Are you lost?" Tryggvi asked curiously. He did not think the cat was wild-born; he may have a touch with creatures, but wild was still wild and were wary of men—even Tryggvi with his elven blood. This creature showed next to no concern—if any at all.

"*I am on an adventure,*" the cat replied haughtily. Tryggvi relayed this to Ásbjörn, who snorted.

"That means yes."

The cat shot Ásbjörn a supercilious glare. Ásbjörn ignored the tiny vessel of wrath and sat down comfortably on the log and rested his chin in a palm to watch the proceedings, scratching Frode's head idly. Frode thumped his tail happily on the ground, letting Ásbjörn's attention sooth his wounded soul.

"Where's your family?" Tryggvi asked next, and the kitten's ears and whiskers drooped.

"*I don't have any.*"

The younger boy's face filled with sadness, and he patted the kitten's head. "I lost my family once, too. But Björn gave me a new family. I could do the same for *you* if you want! Mother likes cats."

"*Of course, I'll be coming with you,*" the kitten informed him haughtily. "*I have already decided. You smell of home, after all.*"

"I do?"

"*Yes.*" The kitten bent its tiny pink nose to Tryggvi's finger, which was still stroking along its back now. "*I can smell it clearly—green and flowers and living things. You've got elven blood.*"

Tryggvi blinked. "So?"

The kitten raised its head and fluffed its tail proudly. "*My people are no ordinary felines. We are the cats of the Elven Forests, the companions of elf-kind. Yes, there's no better place for me. I shall take over your human home, here.*"

Tryggvi was still blinking in surprise, so Ásbjörn asked him what was going on.

"The kitten says that he's going to take over our house?"

"Well, he's a cat,' Ásbjörn said reasonably. "What I expected, really. Well, if he's going to stay, ask him what his name is."

"Good idea!" Tryggvi chirped and turned back to the cat. "What's—"

"*I'm not deaf,*" the kitten sniffed. "*My illustrious name is Allvaldi.*"

"That's a nice name," Tryggvi said. "It's nice to meet you, Allvaldi!"

Ásbjörn started laughing. Both Allvaldi and Tryggvi turned frowns (or whatever a cat's version of a frown is) on him. "It's not nice to make fun of his name, Ásbjörn!"

"No, no," his brother protested, still laughing. "I'm not making fun of his name. I'm just impressed by how perfect it is."

Allvaldi appeared mollified by this and consented to being picked up by Tryggvi. The younger boy tucked him carefully into the folds of his cloak. Once the kitten was secured, Ásbjörn stood up, stretching. "Well, it's getting late. We should be getting back."

"Aww… but we didn't find the palace of Býulfr!" Tryggvi said, his shoulders slumping dejectedly. Frode trotted over, sniffing curiously in an attempt to see where the tiny fluff had gone.

Ásbjörn gently nudged Frode away, then reached out and ruffled his little brother's head. "We still have close to nine months before I leave; we have plenty of time to find it. Besides…" his fingers moved to Allvaldi's nose, an offering for sniffing, "you found a perfectly fine treasure all of your own instead. A good reward for a day's adventure, don't you think?"

Tryggvi cheered up at this, Allvaldi puffed up at the idea of being a treasure, and the four of them made their way home.

They spent the next nine months tromping back and forth through the forest, the four of them: Ásbjörn and Tryggvi, of course, and Frode rushing in circles around them, nose seeking out all the different smells, and Allvaldi digging his little claws into the fabric of Tryggvi's tunic from his perch on the boy's shoulder.

Summer, and autumn, and winter all passed, and by the time spring had begun again, they still had not found the palace of Býulfr, and Ásbjörn was heading off to the mountain.

His family all stood at the gate and said their farewells—a reassuring grasp on the shoulder from King Ólaf, a kiss on the forehead and a blessing from Queen Ljúfvina, and a big, sloppy lick from Frode.

Tryggvi was last, hovering unhappily in the background. He was trying his best not to let his sadness show on his face; he was nine winters now, basically a grown-up, and grown-ups don't pout. He wasn't very successful.

Ásbjörn walked over to him, his traveling pack slung over his shoulder, and Tryggvi gave it a resentful look.

"How now, little brother, why the long face?"

"That's a stupid question," Tryggvi grumped, and Ásbjörn sighed. His little brother stared determinedly down at his toes and the way Allvaldi had decided to drape his magnificent self over them. Because of this, he was startled when a warm, solid weight settled forcefully on his head.

Startled, his gaze darted up to lock with his elder brother's. As soon as their eyes met, Ásbjörn smiled brightly, and ruffled Tryggvi's hair. "Don't worry, little brother. I won't be gone long—but I have a job for you until I come back." His voice leveled and grew serious as he spoke, his gaze locking with Tryggvi's solemnly.

"What kind of job?" Tryggvi asked, a little breathlessly.

"Until I get back, would you take care of being Father's heir? All right?" His hand dropped from Tryggvi's head to sweep out towards everything they could see—the bustle of the village, the height of the mountain, the green of the forest, the wind rushing through the grass, the endless blue stretch of the sea. "Look after our country for me and take care of Mother. It won't be for too long, just until I come home. Would you?"

Tryggvi set his jaw and clenched his fists, nodding firmly. He stuck one hand out, and Ásbjörn clasped it tightly in a warrior's pledge. "I'll take care of it all!" he swore in a voice that he imagined was deep and heroic, but as he was nine, it came out rather squeakily. "So come home soon!"

Ásbjörn grinned. "Thank you." Then he tugged Tryggvi into an embrace, thumping him firmly on the back a few times. Allvaldi yowled in acute displeasure at being disturbed from his chosen couch, but neither heeded him at all. "Don't have too much fun without me!"

"No promises!" Tryggvi replied and stuck out his tongue.

His brother laughed, and then stepped back, crouching down in front of Frode. The dog's normally curled tail was drooping, clearly sensing something was amiss. Ásbjörn rubbed a hand up and down Frode's neck, scratching here and there. "Frode, I can't take you with me, so stay with Tryggvi, and help him look after everyone for me? Be a good boy and stay here and take care of them until I get back."

Tryggvi crouched down beside Frode and flung his arms around the dog's neck and whispered the message into his black, pointed ear. Then he grinned up at Ásbjörn and winked. "He'll take good care of us!"

Ásbjörn winked back and ruffled Frode's ears happily and was rewarded with another sloppy caress to the cheek.

Allvaldi smacked Tryggvi's leg with one clawed paw. *Tell your brother that dwarves are boring, so he'd better hurry back. I won't stand it if he comes back yammering about rocks all the time.*

Tryggvi obediently whispered this in Ásbjörn's ear, who smiled.

"Thank you, master Allvaldi," he said solemnly. "I'll keep that in mind." He reached down to stroke Allvaldi's ears, and the cat condescended to allow it.

After a couple scritches, Ásbjörn gave both Frode and Tryggvi a head ruffle, and stood up.

"All right, Master Thekkr, I'm ready to go!"

The dwarf standing by the gate smiled and nodded, hefting his own travel pack over his shoulder before bowing his head to the royal family. "My father will take good care of him, your majesties. There's no need to worry."

"Thank you, Master Thekkr," Ólaf replied, and Ljúfvina smiled faintly in the swell of reassurance.

The dwarf turned his attention to his charge. "Very well now, lad. Let's be off!"

The two of them set out upon the road, but they had barely gone two score paces before Ásbjörn paused and turned back a moment to wave. "Good-bye, everyone! Try not to miss me too much—I'll be back in a year and a day, so see you soon!"

Then he turned his face back towards the mountain and hurried to catch up with his guide.

Tryggvi wrapped his arms around Frode and pressed his face into the thick grey fur. It was soft and warm against his face, and the fluff of cat curled about his feet and the two pairs of hands on his shoulders were just as warm.

I miss him already, though.

I can't wait till he comes back home.

CHAPTER 5

It was a bright day in high summer, the leaves on the trees dark and glossy green, the sun shining brightly in a bright blue sky dotted with clouds as white and fluffy as sheep's wool, and Rósfrída could hardly contain herself.

"Come on, come on, let's goooo!"

If there ever was an incarnation of excitement itself, Ingiborg mused with a smile from where she sat at her work, *it would be Rósfrída right now.*

Svanhilda was not particularly interested in running wild on the mountain, while that was fairly all Rósfrída was interested in. Instead, Svanhilda liked learning to make things—sewing and spinning and how to tastefully arrange beads in a bracelet from her mother, and how to carve from her father. And, since Rósfrída and Svanhilda were supposed to stick together, the younger usually was restricted to running about near their house, within earshot. This was not very exciting when there was a whole rest of a mountain to explore.

But today was different; today Svanhilda, noticing Rósfrída's increasingly wistful glances towards the woods beyond their grove, had proposed a plan. It was high summer, after all—and the lingonberries were ripe. So Rósfrída's excitement was threefold, not only with the prospect of an adventure with Svanhilda, but the promise of lingonberry jam and *lingonpäron* in the future.

"I thought you were ready to leave!" Rósfrída pleaded, swinging herself impatiently on the doorframe. Svanhilda looked up from where she was tightening the ankle-lace of her boot and shared a fond grin with her mother.

"I'm coming, Rósfrída!" Svanhilda laughed. "I just don't want to run about barefoot on the mountain, like *someone*, that's all."

Rósfrída articulately portrayed her thoughts on this argument by scrunching her nose and sticking out her tongue. It was a failed attack, as it only made Svanhilda giggle, and did nothing to her hurry her progress. Still, only a minute later, Svanhilda pulled the knot of her other boot firm and stood up, gathering her basket. "You ready to go?"

Rósfrída was fairly vibrating in place. "*Yesssssss!*"

Svanhilda grinned, Rósfrída's excitement being of the contagious sort. And it wasn't that Svanhilda *didn't* like to be outside; she just liked other things more. Still, there was a constant cool breeze rustling the leaves and carrying the green smell of summer, and Svanhilda realized she had missed the wild, too. Certainly not as much as Rósfrída, however.

"All right, then. Let's go! Bye, Mama."

"Bye, Mama!" Rósfrída shouted with a wave, and then was out of the clearing like a shot.

Svanhilda rolled her eyes and broke into a sprint after her. "Wait up, Rósfrída! I'm not as fast as you are, and you know that!"

They spent the afternoon running up and down on the mountain, hunting out the best patches and picking as many berries as they could. They had nothing to fear on the mountain, for it was their grandfather's and covered in his power; the mountain would protect them. Rósfrída flitted all around the patches, like a butterfly wandering around a meadow, while Svanhilda picked a spot and worked steadily. It wasn't long before their stomachs were full and their hands stained red with juice, but it was a bit longer until their baskets were full.

Svanhilda was lost in the rhythm of berry-picking, and only looked up when Rósfrída tugged her sleeve nervously. "Svana? I don't like the sky."

Svanhilda blinked up at the sky and frowned. She didn't like it herself, though she wasn't as good at reading the wind and the heavens as Rósfrída. Dark, heavy clouds were blowing in from the sea, and the earlier breeze had turned chill and harsh. At that moment a distant rumble echoed through the air, and Svanhilda bit her lip. The clouds were moving faster than she'd like, and they had wandered a good way away from home. Even if the mountain was kindly towards them, that was no reason to tempt fate by wandering blindly on it in a storm.

"There's a grove nearby, right?" Svanhilda mused, thinking hard. It'd been a while since she'd last had a roam on the mountain with Rósfrída; something she was regretting now. "We'll go there and wait out the storm."

"Hooray!" Rósfrída cheered, her worry instantly fleeing from the combined assault of her faith in her big sister and the prospect before her. "It'll be like camping! Let's go!"

And she was off like a shot, bouncing and skipping between the bushes, heading towards the grove. Svanhilda shook head and hefted her basket, but there was a grin on her face as she set off after Rósfrída. Trust her little sister to see the bright side in any situation.

Rósfrída was hovering excitedly at the edge of the grove when her elder sister caught up. "Look, there's a path here!" she said, pointing at the ground.

Svanhilda tapped the ground with her foot curiously. It was definitely a path, even if it was faint. She could feel the presence of someone or something crossing back and forth over the earth and stone over a long time.

"If we follow it, Svana, maybe we can find someplace to stay!" Rósfrída said excitedly.

Svanhilda shook her head slightly with an exasperated grin. "You can't follow every path and stick your nose into everything, Rósfrída. You never know what you might find."

"But it's grandfather's mountain," Rósfrída said, blinking. "There's nothing bad here. Papa and Mama and Grandfather say so!"

Svanhilda had to concede the point, but she remembered the stories Papa told of his voyages on the sea, or Grandfather's tales of mountains tall and dark. She made a note to ask Grandfather to tell some of those stories the next time they saw him.

Still, Rósfrída was right—at least on this mountain, it was safe. What's more, it was worth a try. "All right, let's go and see what we can find."

They ducked into the grove just as the first raindrops came pelting down from the sky.

The path wound in and out about the trees, as if the one who made it had once wandered through the grove aimlessly and then proceeded to tread that path every day for years and years.

Finally, they came to the end of the path, right up against a cliffside, but there was a tree growing there, roots spread out stubbornly over a hollow in the rock that had been worn away by the years. It created a nice little shelter, the roots intertwined tightly as a basket. Below, the ground was covered with soft, thick moss. A little rivulet trickled its way out and away into the darkness cast by the storm, tinkling so softly it could not be heard over the sound of the rain pounding against the leaves.

"Quick, in here!" Svanhilda said, and snatching up her sister's hand, they scurried inside together.

It was clean and dry, and actually rather roomy, though of course neither girl was very big or took up much space. They huddled on the nice thick moss, their backs against the cool stone, and waited. The rain pounded on the stone and on the tree roots overhead, a soft, drumming never-ending rhythm. Slowly, slowly, it lulled both the children to sleep, safe in the arms of the mountain.

Svanhilda's sleep was restless, however—full of darkness and sorrow and unease. In her dreams the mountain shook and cried out in pain, and there was nothing she could do to make it better.

It was morning when Svanhilda stirred and blinked open her eyes to find a little boy crouched in front of them, hands on his knees and head tilted curiously.

"Ah, you're awake!" he said, a smile crossing his face.

Svanhilda blinked, rubbing at her eyes. "Who are you?" It wasn't perhaps the politest way to greet somebody, but Svanhilda had just woken up and was rather confused, and she had never seen this boy before.

He wasn't very big, not much younger than her for certain, with green eyes and flaxen-pale hair feathering about his shoulders. "My name is Eylir, and welcome to my grove!"

"Your grove?" Svanhilda looked curiously at the trees outside of their little nook. "What makes this your grove?"

"Oh, that's simple," Eylir said, nodding confidently. "I was born here, so that makes it mine. To look after and care for. Mother told me so!"

Svanhilda nodded sagely, for that made sense. Mothers were very wise, after all, so if Eylir's mother told him that, then it must be true. "Thank you for your hospitality," she said, bowing her head solemnly.

"My pleasure! That is what groves are for, after all," the boy said, and then shuffled back and stood up. "It's tomorrow already, so your mother is probably waiting for you. You should go and see her as soon as you can!"

So Svanhilda coaxed Rósfrída into wakefulness, though Rósfrída protested mightily. Still, at last Svanhilda's little sister was on her feet, even if her eyes were still screwed shut against the morning's brightness and she clung to Svanhilda's hand tightly.

"Follow me, just like you did last night," Eylir said as he stepped out of their shelter. "With last night's rain the ground will be even more unsafe."

Svanhilda was startled. "Last night? We didn't see you last night."

"No, you wouldn't have; I wasn't here," Eylir replied. "But I felt people in my grove, and you have to be careful here. Look!"

He pointed to one side, and there, some dozen feet away, the ground dropped off into a steep cliff. Svanhilda gasped and reflexively tugged Rósfrída closer to her side.

"But my will and spirit are in these trees, so I guided you along a safe path to a place of shelter," Eylir explained. "But Mother says it's rude for a host to not show his face, so I came over to say hello this morning and send you on your way."

Svanhilda gathered up her nerves, which had been badly shaken at seeing the cliff. The mountain was kind and cared for them, but even the mountain could not do much if they wandered off its edge. "Thank you, again, for looking out for us! We couldn't see the cliff in the dark."

The boy puffed out his chest happily, looking pleased. "I'm glad to help! That's what my people do, after all."

Svanhilda bowed her head once more, and then set off towards home, tugging a very sleepy Rósfrída along behind her. Just before they left the grove, however, Eylir called out to them one last time.

"Be careful on your way back!" he shouted; his face worried. "Something has happened on this mountain. I can't understand the stones, but the trees tell me the mountain is very sad."

Very sad? Suddenly, Svanhilda remembered her dream, and the knot of unease twisted itself back into existence in her stomach. What had happened to make the mountain cry like that?

"We'll be careful!" she called back, and with a final wave, she and Rósfrída set off towards home.

The moment they approached their house, however, Ingiborg rushed out, falling to her knees in front of her children and wrapping them in her arms, holding them tight and close. "Oh, you're safe! Thank the Wanderer!"

"Mama? Is somethin' wrong?" Rósfrída piped up curiously, but Svanhilda found she couldn't speak, the knot in her stomach rising to lodge in her throat.

"I don't know, child," their mother sighed. "But something is wrong with the mountain, and when you didn't come home last night… your father is out there looking for you. Where were you?"

Svanhilda managed to swallow the lump in her throat and explained what had happened. At the end, Ingiborg drew back, looking faintly relieved.

"You must have met an elf-child," she said, "for those people are charged by the Lee of Flame to guard over the forests, and to watch over those that are lost within the woods, especially children. The hand of the Wanderer must have been on you, that you stumbled upon an elven-grove. I wasn't aware there were any on this mountain."

"What's an elfen-gove?" Rósfrída asked, tugging curiously on Ingiborg's skirt. Her mother looked down at her youngest fondly, smoothing her hand along the girl's bright red hair.

"An elven-grove is a grove where an elf was born. When the time comes for an elf mother to give birth, she lets her heart lead her to a grove where the child wishes to be born, and that grove is ever after in the care of that child. Those places are blessed and filled with good and kind power. It was indeed the kindness of Highest Heaven you found a place like that."

"Oooh," Rósfrída said, very impressed, though Svanhilda wondered how much she really understood. Still, Rósfrída had another question ready as she always did, and Ingiborg led her children back to the house, answering all her youngest's questions with all the patience of stone. Svanhilda listened curiously, but she couldn't quite get rid of the nagging unease, and she wondered why the mountain was sad.

She wouldn't find out until nearly five days later, when Mama's brother Nefir arrived and brought the news. There had been an accident of some kind, and Grandfather, Granduncle, and their student had all died.

The whole of the city of the Folkbiörn was in mourning, for ill news had arrived. Fáinn the dwarf, son of Alvíss, had come down from the mountains with the tidings that something had happened on Alvíss' mountain—some pulse of power, an accident that had felled the dwarf and his brother… and Prince Ásbjörn, who was studying underneath the tutelage of that dwarf.

Queen Ljúfvina had shut herself in her closet. King Ólaf sat on his throne, silent and stone-faced.

The younger prince Tryggvi took his cat and hid in a tree, staying there until the sun went down and the stars came out. Finally, an hour after the sun went down, he spoke, staring off at the mountains between the branches of the pine tree.

"They say he's dead, but they don't have any proof. Just that they felt the power pulse, and that the mountain was sad, and when they looked the dwarves and Ásbjörn were gone. But… but if there isn't a body, that means he could be alive, right?"

Allvaldi leaned his small body against Tryggvi's leg, silent.

"Right, Allvaldi?" Tryggvi repeated, in a whisper.

'I don't know.'

Tryggvi felt his chest lurch, and he bit his lip to hold back the sob that desperately wanted to be let out. He'd been left before, by Mama and Papa a long time ago; he could barely remember their faces now. Would a day come when he couldn't remember Ásbjörn's face?

He dug his fingernails into the tree bark, feeling the sticky resin of pine cling to his fingers and palms. "He can't be dead. He… he promised he'd be back soon, and Ásbjörn doesn't break his promises. He… he *wouldn't*."

The cat stirred, clearly searching for something to say. *'Your brother… hold on, is that the dog?'*

Tryggvi blinked and peered down at the base of the tree. Frode was sitting there, staring up into the boughs.

The boy quickly scrambled down, and Allvaldi followed him, though the cat declined to descend fully to the ground, but instead remained on the lowest branch, peering down superciliously at the dog below. Tryggvi crouched in front of the dog, however, and flung his arms around Frode's fluffy neck.

"Do you miss him, boy?" he whispered into the thick grey fur. "I do too. I wish… I wish he'd come home."

'I saw Master. He says he misses you, but he can't come home.'

Tryggvi blinked. He blinked again. Then he jerked back with a gasp, a multitude of emotions he couldn't quite figure out rising in his chest like a thunderhead.

"Ásbjörn? You saw big brother?"

Frode licked his cheek, sensing the boy's turmoil. *'Sort of. He looked different and smelled a little odd, but it was still Master.'*

What? Tryggvi wasn't sure what that meant, but he *did* know one thing.

Ásbjörn was *alive*. He hadn't broken his promise. But something had happened to him, something that meant he couldn't come home.

That was all right. That just meant it was up to Tryggvi, instead. And if he looked different, well, that wouldn't be a problem. After all, he had Mama's special seeing stone.

He wouldn't let anything stop him from finding his brother and bringing him home.

And he would, sure as the mountains and the tides.

>>*<< · >>*<< · >>*<<

A white bear stood on a hill, looking down into the city of the Folkbiörn. His business was complete, so he turned his face toward the mountains and walked away, disappearing into the gloom of the forest.

He no longer had a place amongst the towns and cities of men, after all. It was best if he stayed away.

But he wished he could have seen them all just one more time.

>>*<< · >>*<< · >>*<<

"Hmm. Well, that's interesting," the Wanderer said, his gaze turning westward. "Once again my gift to Farbiörn is used as a curse rather than a blessing."

He sighed heavily, then turned and lifted his staff, calling down the mountain. "Flosi! Come up here, I have an errand for you!"

A blonde head poked through the branches of a holly tree some ways away. "Oh good!" The head disappeared and a few moments later its owner, a tall elf with long braids knotted together at the back of his shoulder blades and a harp cradled in the crook of his arm, appeared. He dashed up the hill and skidded to a halt in front of his companion, an eager grin on his face.

"What sort of task do you have for me, Finnvard? Where do you wish me to wander? I've been having itchy feet of late, so this is welcome indeed!"

The Wanderer watched Flosi with amusement. "I want you to stay on a mountain and watch over it."

Flosi blinked. "Ah."

His tone was considerably less than enthusiastic.

"The mountain happens to be west of here, by the shores of the sea…" The Wanderer eyed his companion carefully as he added, "and near the land of the Folkbiörn."

The change was immediate. "Oh, excellent! A nice long vacation would do me good. When shall I set off, and which mountain in particular?"

The young, the Wanderer mused fondly. *They never change.* "Right away, and to Alvíss' mountain, if you are familiar with it."

At that, Flosi cocked an eyebrow. "I am... the grove of one of my newest brothers is on that mountain. But why... Alvíss is good hearted and respected by all. What need do you have of me to watch it?"

"Because Alvíss is dead."

"Well." Flosi nodded and clicked his tongue. "That would do it." His gaze turned westward, and he cocked his head thoughtfully to one side. "Do you think foul play was involved? Who is responsible?"

The Wanderer hummed. "I am not all-seeing, young Flosi. Those are things I do not know—though I have my suspicions."

The elf eyed his companion curiously. "I see... still, what need do you have of me there? It is a mountain rich with dwarf-power, and I am an elf. Wouldn't it make more sense to send a dwarf?"

"Perhaps... but I am worried. It was kept a secret, but my sources have told me what Alvíss was working on—a special vault for the king of the Folkbiörn: a pocket of land hidden within a mirror. I am sure you are aware of the dangers of meddling with mirrors."

Flosi's mouth tightened at this. "Mirrors reflect their masters. If Alvíss died by foul play—"

"Exactly." The Wanderer peered off into the west underneath the wide brim of his hat. "Alvíss had a good heart, and that would have been embedded in his work. Still, mirrors are particularly susceptible, and if something is not done... Well. I for one do *not* wish to have a repeat of last time."

"I should say not!" Flosi laughed, but the tone of his laughter was strained. "Still... I am glad to help, but what am I supposed to do, compared to anyone else?"

The Wanderer leaned heavily on his staff. "As to why *you* instead of a dwarf? A dwarf's power lies in the making of things. I am going for *subtle,* and a dwarf coming in with a hammer is not that. I do not wish to meddle with the mirror, only keep it safe for now."

"But... the power of a dwarf and the power of an elf are antithesis to each other!" Flosi flapped his hands, exasperated. "Dwarves are earth and stone and metal, while my people are grass and flowers and trees!"

The Wanderer smiled, a twinkle in his eye. "But do not grass and flowers and trees grow from the ground?"

Flosi paused, blinking, and bit his lip, considering it.

"Secondly, because of your travels and your... apprenticeship, shall we say, you are skilled at intermingling your power with that of others. You should be able to guide and guard the power of the mirror and keep it safe, slipping in between the cracks of Alvíss' power to do so. No one else can do such a job."

The elf stared for a long, long moment, before finally nodding. "I don't know if I quite have the faith in myself that you seem to have in me... but nothing ventured, nothing gained! I shall do my best, though I doubt that will be enough."

"That is all I ask," the Wanderer said.

"Besides," Flosi said, brightening, "I shall be able to spend time with Eylir, so that should be fun! I *have* missed him and home."

The Wanderer laughed. "I am certain your brother and your home are not the only things you have missed, but yes."

"Finnvard, your eye sees too much," Flosi laughed in return. "Bards are supposed to have an air of mystery, you know."

"It only counts as a mystery if you do a fair job of hiding it," his companion returned. "But go. I am sure your *brother* will be happy to see you."

Flosi grinned and turned to go, lifting one hand.

The Wanderer raised his in return, smiling fondly. "Now farewell, until our paths cross again."

CHAPTER 6

Rósfrída was antsy. It was a beautiful spring day on the mountain, the snows having melted away at last, leaving the entire mountainside draped in a cloak of flowers and brilliant green.

And she couldn't go out and enjoy it.

"I can't go outside with you, Rósfrída," Svanhilda said sternly. "I have to take care of mother."

Rósfrída sucked in a deep breath and held it. Mother was ill, and Svanhilda was taking care of her, and being trapped in the house while Mother lay so still and quiet on her bed made Rósfrída's feet itch to move. To run to somewhere where she could close her eyes and imagine Mother smiling and laughing and not hear any coughs to break her image.

Ingiborg had never been strong. She had been born early, and with more of her mother's human blood than her father's dwarf. When she had been young, a sickness seeped into her lungs, and ever after the deep airs of her family's home and the smokes off the forge were too much for her.

Ingiborg could no longer participate in the craft of her people, nor stay in their land, not if she wished to live. So, Alvíss picked out a mountain by the margins of the sea, where the air was clean and fresh, and the sea wind blew life into her lungs. There he had built a house for his daughter and wrapped the mountain with his power to keep her safe.

And there, by the edge of the sea, Ingiborg had met a traveling merchant—a man who followed the winds across the seas.

But even the high and sea airs, even the power of Alvíss that still lingered after his death, could not entirely protect Ingiborg. It hadn't happened often, but sometimes an ill wind blew and Ingiborg would take to her bed. Kiúli had gone to the nearest village to get medicine, Svanhilda was taking care of Mother, and Rósfrída was restless.

"Then, can I go by myself?"

Both girls paused at this suggestion. Neither of them had ever considered such a notion before, and neither were quite sure what to do.

Svanhilda took a long, long look at her sister, and saw the itch and restlessness in her limbs, and finally sighed. "If you promise to be careful, and stay close…"

Rósfrída nodded eagerly.

Svanhilda sighed again, and smiled, patting Rósfrída's head. "Then, I suppose."

"Hurrah!"

Rósfrída immediately turned on her heel and bolted for the door, feeling the itch already beginning to leave her feet.

"Be back *well* before sunset, all right?" Svanhilda called after her. "And it's still chilly, so don't forget your coat!"

Rósfrída giggled, too giddy with the prospect of freedom to speak, so she waved a hand in response and swerved to one side, snatching her cloak from the hook before bolting out the door.

Svanhilda shook her head with a wry smile, then glanced over at Ingiborg to see if their noise had disturbed her. Luckily, their mother still slept deeply, though her breathing was somewhat wheezy.

The girl smiled and turned to pick up her drop spindle. She might as well get some of her own particular brand of leisure in while watching mother, as the house was already swept and it would be awhile before she needed to start on a meal.

Svanhilda hummed as she snapped her wrist smoothly, keeping a careful eye on the woolen thread she was spinning. Her shoulders relaxed, and she smiled, humming a little louder.

I hope Rósfrída is having a good time; she's been cooped up in the house for too long.

Rósfrída was having a great time. The sun was shining brightly on the new green of the leaves, a nice, cool wind kept her from getting too warm in her cloak, and she could hear birds singing.

Where should she go? It would have to be a good spot, someplace she'd like to stay and play in, because she promised to stay close and shouldn't wander. Still, she couldn't pick, so she closed her eyes, pointed, and spun quickly in a circle. Then she opened her eyes and trotted off in that direction to find the nearest fun spot.

The first place she found was a little pond and waterfall. It wasn't a particularly high waterfall, but it was wide, and the pool was neither especially large nor deep. It was a good pool to go paddling in, and it was often that their father would take the girls here in the summer. Now, though, spring was still new, and the water was freezing from the snowmelt, so Rósfrída contented herself by looking for pretty stones and pebbles by the shore.

Slowly, she combed her way all along to the cliff's edge, where she ran out of beach to search. Her pouch was now comfortably heavy and bumped softly against her leg whenever she moved. But the sun was still high, high in the blue heaven, and Rósfrída's feet still wanted to move. She sighed, turning around to look for something to do—but as she turned, something caught the corner of her eye.

A shadow behind the falling water, and a little path leading along the edge of the cliff.

An opportunity to explore, without having to go any further away from home? It was exactly what Rósfrída had been looking for! So she tucked the last of her pebbles into her pouch and skipped over to the little ledge along the cliff wall. Now that she was closer, she could see it was wider than she thought, wide enough for a dwarf to walk on, and therefore plenty big enough for a small girl. Still, Rósfrída could *hear* Svanhilda telling her to 'be careful', so Rósfrída took her time walking across the ledge, easing herself along the cliff wall until she slid *behind* the waterfall and into the cave behind.

It was lighter inside than she thought it might be, for the sun was shining on the waterfall. The light broke and refracted on the endlessly falling curtain, sending sparks and dots and fractals of gold and white and rainbow light spinning and dancing throughout the cave. It was a truly lovely sight, made all the lovelier by the fact that so much of the light was caught by something shiny on the far wall and cast back on the floor, making the room twice as bright as it might have been otherwise.

Rósfrída's mouth hung open in awe. Did *all* waterfalls have such pretty places behind them? She needed to look behind more waterfalls!

But first, she should look at whatever the shining thing was on the far wall. It was a little hard to see, with the strange blend of dazzles and shadows, so Rósfrída trotted forward to get a better look.

It was a mirror.

This might have seemed strange, but Rósfrída was only ten, and had dwarven blood in her, what's more. She'd grown up on stories about all sorts of interesting things you might find in caves, so a mirror seemed rather tame by comparison—even if it was a very pretty mirror.

And a pretty mirror it was, not convex like Mama's mirror, but flat, and so much bigger! It seemed, somehow, to be a part of the stone of the wall, but the edges of the mirror were lined out with carvings. All sorts of interesting carvings—of men, and dwarves, and elves, and swords, and dragons and such things, but most especially bears. At the very top, in fact, right in the center, two bears stood, back-to-back, snarling protectively.

Rósfrída couldn't decide what she liked looking at the most: the smooth surface of the glass, or the wonderful, intricate carvings, or her own reflection, which she'd never seen so big and clear before. She stared at it, at how pretty and ethereal she seemed surrounded by the dancing flecks of rainbow light cast by the waterfall behind her. The flecks of light were strangely mesmerizing, drawing the eye to the mirror, pulling the gaze to follow the patterns.

Rósfrída blinked.

She hadn't noticed before now, but she could almost, *almost* see the light on the mirror's surface shining on something *else*. She looked behind her.

The cave was empty, nothing besides the odd patch of dampness and moss on the floor behind her. But… when she looked in the mirror, she could have sworn she saw the light glint off something golden and shiny!

There it was again!

Rósfrída pressed her hands against the glass, trying to get closer to see what it was—

And then she tripped, and slipped, and the gold was there in front of her. A lot of gold.

A king's treasure-worth of it.

There were all sorts of wonders, the majority being items made of gold and silver and jewels: coins and necklaces, plates and goblets, crowns and rings and torques. But there were other treasures there, too, namely a grand variety of weapons: axes, swords, daggers, and shields, and full sets of armor lining the walls. There were many kinds of great hunting trophies: ivory and furs and heads of animals, and a great many drinking horns, gilded and carved and decorated. There were scrolls, too, and stone tablets carved with pictures and runes.

On many of the treasures Rósfrída could sense power. She wasn't as good at it as Svana, because Svana's feet were grounded while Rósfrída chased after the wind, and the power of Ingiborg's people ran thin within her. Still, there was enough that she could taste it, powerful threads that twined about certain items. Most of the power felt like dwarf, but some felt like Eylir their elf-friend, and some was strange and unknown and felt *foreign*. Like some of the wares Papa would buy in his voyages and bring back to sell.

Rósfrída stared with wonder, then excitement stirred in her chest. She turned around, because she had to go get Svana, because such a wonderful discovery as *this* was something that must be shared--

Rósfrída slammed into glass and fell back onto the ground.

>>*<< · >>*<< · >>*<<

In a forest glade on the mountain, a song stuttered to a halt—the strings of a lap-harp twanging discordantly when the player's fingers seized upon them.

A feeling of foreboding latched onto the heart of Flosi the bard; cold fingers digging in mercilessly.

Something was *wrong*. Something was terribly, *terribly* wrong. What, though, and why, he could hardly understand, for he'd built layers of protection all around the entrance to the vault, so he'd be well warned if a malicious or even foreign presence trespassed where it ought not.

So, who had gotten into the treasure-hoard of the Folkbiörn?

He darted over to his pack, digging through it frantically until he found what he sought—a small mirror—and sang the song of the mountain. Something he'd learned once he came here and began poking his nose into the flow of power on the mountain was that Alvíss had somehow bound his little pocket inside the mirror to the mountain's whole. It was quite clever, a way for a guard to observe who approached the vault. If an intruder's reflection was caught in the surface of a stream, or in the polished flat of his own sword, the guard would be able to see and know and prepare.

The loophole was that if you had access to the power—as Flosi himself did—or, clear eyes that saw the truth of things, whatever reflections dwelt upon the mountain would also be laid bare to you, if you simply glanced in a mirror.

So Flosi took out his little looking-glass and bent his mind upon the vault, to see who *dared*—oh.

Oh.

Oh, no.

Flosi very carefully set the mirror down, and just as carefully curled his fingers into his hair and pulled, gritting his teeth against the knot of emotion and noise that swelled in his throat.

Something was definitely wrong—and he wasn't sure how to fix it.

Rósfrída curled up on pile of furs, wrapping her arms around her legs and tugging her knees close to her chest.

She sniffled quietly.

No matter how hard she'd pushed herself against the wall, it refused to let her out at all! She'd tried kicking, and hitting, and even throwing stuff at it, but nothing worked! And now she was hungry and tired and cold, and she just knew Svanhilda would be worried, and when Papa got back with the medicine, he'd be disappointed that Rósfrída was causing trouble when Mama was sick.

Plus… it was awfully lonely in here. It'd been fun to explore by herself, free to wander without worrying about leaving Svanhilda behind… but being stuck in one room, even a very special one full of treasure, is a very different matter than being a few minutes' walk away from Svanhilda's company and hugs.

She sniffled again. Why couldn't she get out? She got in, after all.

At least the walls were interesting. They were made out of glass, too, but in them she could see shapes and scenes flashing by—a glimpse of a tree here, the clear blue sky there, and for a second, she thought she saw a face; but it was gone the next second, replaced by a great white bear.

Rósfrída stopped sniffling, staring in awe. The longer she looked, the bigger the bear seemed to get.

Only when the glass in front of her *rippled* like the surface of a pond did Rósfrída realize this meant the white bear was coming in.

Rósfrída had never seen a bear in person, herself, but her papa had told her very sternly to stay away from them, because they were very, very dangerous.

"Stay away from them, little flower," he'd said. "If you see one, run far, far away, and hope they don't notice you."

Well, it had noticed her. It had stopped halfway through the door and was staring at her with wide eyes.

Well, Rósfrída couldn't run far away. She'd already *tried* that, not to mention the bear was standing in the door.

There was only one other option; a story her Uncle Kili had told her from one of his wanderings in the mountains. So, she grabbed the first thing she could—a cane with gilded carvings—and brought it down as hard as she could on the bear's nose.

"GO AWAY, MISTER BEAR!"

"Ow!" said the bear, and one of its paws came up to cover its nose. "That hurt!"

Rósfrída stared. Papa had told her stories about talking animals before, but she'd never met one herself. Then her nerves overcame her curiosity, and she backed against one wall, holding the cane out in front of her. After all, Papa had said that just because an animal talks, doesn't mean it's good and not dangerous.

She held her cane up higher and raised her shoulders, puffing out her chest in an attempt to look bigger and scarier. "Are you a bad bear, Mister Bear?"

The bear blinked at her and lowered its paw to the ground. "I should hope not. I try very hard to be a good bear."

Rósfrída lowered her cane a little. "Are you a dangerous bear, Mister Bear?"

"All bears are dangerous," the bear said solemnly. "But I don't hurt little girls."

The cane went up again. "I'm a *big* girl, though! Do you hurt big girls?"

The bear huffed a laugh. "No, not big girls, either. Only bad people, who do bad things."

"Oh." Rósfrída considered this. "All right." With that, she lowered her cane. "Do you want to be friends, Mister Bear?"

The bear huffed again, but bowed his great, white head gently. "I would like that very much, miss."

Rósfrída beamed. "All right, Mister Bear. It's nice to meet you! I'm Rósfrída."

"It is nice to meet you, Rósfrída," the bear said, and tilted his head. "You can call me Björn."

The girl burst out into giggles. "That's a very silly name for a bear."

Björn huffed for a third time, but his eyes seemed a little sad. "So it is. I can't help that, though."

"Well, it's very nice to meet you, Mister Björn, but I'mma little stuck." She skipped forward hopefully, standing in front of his nose, resisting the urge to pet it. "Can you help me get out?"

"I can certainly try," Björn replied, and lay down to be a bit more on the girl's level. "How did you get in?"

"I'm not really sure," the girl replied, waving her arms helplessly. Her cane nearly missed beaning Björn on the nose again. "I was looking into the mirror and I just… *fell?* That's pretty much all that happened."

The bear hummed thoughtfully. "And you can't get out?"

Prickling warmth welled up behind Rósfrída's eyes; she tried valiantly to keep her lip from wobbling. "I tried."

"Well," Björn said, "there's nothing for it but to try again. I come in and out all the time, so I don't see why you shouldn't. Why don't you climb on my back and see if you can come through with me?"

Rósfrída brightened at this. Her excitement was not only due to the hope of freedom, but to the prospect of riding on the back of a bear, which had its own irresistible appeal. "All right! Let's do that!"

So Björn stood up and finished walking into the chamber, and then turned around, lowering himself to the ground for easier access. "Climb on, then, and let us see if we can get you out."

Rósfrída gleefully scrambled up onto his back, settling behind his shoulder blades and sinking her hands deep into his soft, thick fur.

"All set, little one?" the bear rumbled, his deep voice vibrating against his chest. Rósfrída could feel it against her legs and hands, and she giggled. "Ready!"

Björn lowered his head and set his gaze on the mirror, shoulders bunching in focus and determination. Then, he pushed forward. His nose went through, then his head, then his shoulders—before it came to an abrupt *stop*, just as soon as the mirror glass touched Rósfrída's hands.

Rósfrída's heart froze just as Björn's movements did.

This wasn't good. What did one do when one's "try again" failed, too?

Svanhilda was getting worried; it was starting to get late. Papa should be back soon, but Rósfrída should have been back hours ago.

Should I wake up Mother? But… Svanhilda bit her lip, fiddling anxiously with her drop spindle. *She finally started to sleep peacefully.*

*Then, should I go out and look myself? But then mother would be left alone…
There's no good answer.*

Maybe I should go out anyway—

There was a pattering sound on the stone walls of the house, and Svanhilda jerked in surprise when it finally trickled down through her senses. She dropped the spindle and her work and rushed to the door.

While Svanhilda had been sitting here thinking, heavy clouds had blown in from the sea, bringing rain with them. The raindrops fell in sheets, heavy and blinding, and making travel extremely dangerous.

She immediately slammed the door shut against the wind, and the *boom* it made banged uneasily against her suddenly racing heart. Rósfrída had always been the best at reading the winds, so she would have noticed a storm was coming and come straight back home; they'd been extra careful since the incident three years ago.

Svanhilda leaned her back against the stone wall, wringing her hands nervously.

Unless… she was trapped by the storm? But this time she didn't have anyone with her…

This was all her fault.

Rósfrída was stuck on the mountain, who knows where, and Mama was sick, and Papa—Svanhilda sucked in a breath.

Papa was a merchant and had been traversing the waves since he was but a lad. If Rósfrída was good at feeling out the caprices of the winds, then Kiúli was ten times as good. Surely, he'd noticed a storm was coming and find shelter—but… but what if he couldn't? What if there wasn't time to find someplace safe?

Slowly, Svanhilda slid to the ground and buried her face in her knees, her breaths coming quick and uneven.

Mama was sick.

Papa wasn't here.

Rósfrída was missing.

She was all alone.

Svanhilda had never been alone in her life. When she was very little, either her mother or father had always been around her, and then Rósfrída had been born. Just as Ingiborg had asked, Svanhilda had stuck by her little sister's side. Then, even if Papa had to go on a voyage, or Mama was feeling ill that day, she'd had someone to stand by her side, cheering her on.

But now she knew what solitude felt like, and it was a yawning, empty void, echoing and cold.

Her breaths came faster, and she tried to curl even tighter into herself, trying to chase away the cold—

There was a thump against the door.

The girl instantly scrambled to her feet and raced towards the door, her heart rising in her throat along with her hope. Was it Papa? Had he made it home despite the rain? Or even Rósfrída—

She flung the door open, eyes wide and glimmering with relief.

Her eyes became wider and less relieved the next moment, for she found herself face-to-face with neither her father nor her little sister, but a great white bear.

"Excuse me, miss," the bear said politely, as water ran down his nose and plinked onto the floor, "but would you happen to be Svanhilda Ingiborgardottir?"

Svanhilda blinked. It was certainly not every day that a bear showed up at the door to your cottage in the middle of a rainstorm, asking for you by name. Still, Ingiborg had taught her daughters well, and the demands and laws of hospitality were well ingrained in Svanhilda, particularly.

"Oh, uh, yes. I am she." Her voice stuttered slightly, but she took a deep breath. Mama had told her that they might someday have magical creatures as guests, for between her vast passel of siblings, her father's renown, and Kiúli's voyaging, their family had quite widespread connections. The most important thing for her to remember with such creatures was to be cautious but polite, and not to let nerves get the best of her. She pondered her options carefully. Mama was sick, and Papa wasn't back yet...

But the poor creature looked rather miserable, its fur matted and soaked, streaks of mud marring what must have once been a pristine white coat. Mama had also said hospitality was important, and she couldn't ignore someone in need!

Well, there was one thing she could do. "Would you like to come in, Mr. Bear? We'd be very pleased to have you as our guest."

With that delivered, some of her confidence returned, her

shoulders straightening as her chin rose.

A talking bear was surely a magical creature of some sort, and if non-magical people regarded the laws of hospitality with great importance, how much more would a talking bear? As her guest, he wouldn't be able to do anything to hurt her, not without risking retribution from those that safekept such laws.

"Thank you, kind little host," the bear rumbled, and managed to squeeze his way in through the door. Svanhilda closed it tight against the wind once he was through. Then there was a bear standing sheepishly just inside their threshold, with enough rain dripping off him to make it seem like he'd brought his own personal raincloud inside the house with him.

"Oh!" Svanhilda cried in consternation. She'd have to get fresh straw for the floor—but the first order of business was to find something big enough to towel a bear. Maybe a blanket?... "Stay right there; I'll come back with something to help!"

She eventually found a blanket that needed to be mended, and with that she set about toweling off as much of the water as she could. The bear obligingly stayed still and let the slip of a girl bustle about him with impressive equanimity. Finally, she was done, and her blanket was damp and grimy and covered in white hair, but the bear was still not entirely dry. Svanhilda frowned thoughtfully.

"Why don't you come over by the fire and lie there? That should help, right?"

The bear dipped his head gratefully. "I thank you again; that should do quite nicely."

He shuffled his way carefully over to the fireplace and settled down. Svanhilda trailed after him curiously and took a seat nearby— but not too close, just in case.

"What's your name, Mister Bear, and why are you looking for me?"

The bear lifted his head, and something in his eyes struck the girl. For one thing, they were not black or brown like she'd expect from most animals, but blue like a midnight sky, and they seemed rather sad.

"You may call me Björn, miss," he said, his voice a solemn rumble. "As for the reason I'm here…" His head drooped a little, eyes fixed on the floor. "I come bearing news about your sister."

Svanhilda's head jerked up in shock. "Rósfrída? Why?"

"I'm afraid she is stuck somewhere," Björn replied, "and she can't quite seem to get out."

When Kiuli finally made it home early the next morning, having set out as soon as the sun rose from the cave in which he'd hunkered down halfway up the mountain during the storm, he was greeted by a rather unusual—and perhaps even disconcerting—sight.

Namely, his wife and eldest daughter had been crying, his youngest was missing, and there was a bear napping in front of his fire.

Kiúli, however, was a man used to sailing the ever-changing and unpredictable seas and knew how to keep his head and feet level when waves rocked his ship. So, he took a deep breath and examined the situation.

While his wife and daughter were clearly distressed, this distress did *not* seem particularly linked to the bear. Very well. The bear could be ignored for now; what was important was Rósfrída.

His wife had fallen asleep again, and Svanhilda hadn't noticed him come in, too busy being hunched in a miserable huddle in the bed she shared with her sister. So her father quietly walked across the floor and shook her shoulder gently to rouse her.

She stirred and looked up at the touch. As soon as she saw him standing there, her eyes widened, and the sobs she had been holding back finally managed to escape.

"Papa!"

The word tore from her throat, loud and raw and wailing, wracked with sadness. Thin arms wrapped tightly about Kiúli's waist, and his daughter buried her face in his chest, weeping.

A lump rose in Kiúli's throat, the special brand of helplessness that came whenever one of his girls cried, and he gently patted her back and stroked her hair, trying to calm her. The bear watched from the fireplace, clear intelligence shining in its oddly blue eyes. He was distracted from thoughts of the bear, however, because the noise of Svanhilda's crying was enough to wake Ingiborg. She stirred listlessly, and her eyes blinked open to take in the sight of her husband with his arms full of crying daughter.

"Kiúli!" she gasped, and staggered to her feet before he could stop her. Her face was pale and her hair hung wild and loose, and the skin beneath her eyes was red and raw. "Husband!"

As gently as he could, Kiúli shifted Svanhilda to one side and opened one arm to his wife, and she stumbled across the room and fell into his chest. Now that she was by his side, Kiúli could hear the wheezing rattle in her breaths, and his heart clenched with fear.

Whatever had happened? "What's wrong, love?" he asked, reaching up to cradle her head against his shoulder. His breath hitched as he asked the next question. "Where's Rósfrída?"

Of course, Rósfrída was a free spirit and was very like him as a child, but he doubted very much she would run off while Svanhilda and Ingiborg were crying, even if she very much wished to. So… if she was not here…

"She's stuck," Ingiborg whispered against his shoulder, "in the vault that Father was making. And I do not know—" Her voice broke, but she gamely mustered the courage to go on. "I had to stop learning too soon to be of any help."

Kiúli could hear the guilt in her voice, and it made his heart ache. He leaned his head against her own, letting his voice drop and soften. "None of that now, love. You didn't send her there, did you?"

There was a beat of silence, then Ingiborg slowly shook her head. Kiúli ran his hand soothingly up and down her shoulder, mulling over his words, picking each one carefully. "Then, it's not your fault. It's just an accident, and no one can help that. Besides," and he somehow managed to pull a faint smile onto his face, despite the fear and panic that was hammering in his chest, "you were always more interested in making jewelry than anything like what Alvíss made that vault from, right?"

A faint laugh, watery and choked, unwillingly bubbled out of Ingiborg's throat, and Kiúli felt a little bit of his panic and anxiety begin to settle. Everything felt like it was swirling out of control, but that wasn't true. If he was able to figure out how to help Ingiborg, then he might be able to figure out how to help Rósfrída, simple as that.

He took a deep breath and let it out, tapping his fingers one after another on Svanhilda's shoulder, just like he'd done when she was a baby and couldn't sleep from colic. It seemed to do the trick, and her sobbing began to die down.

He breathed in and out again, closing his eyes. He just needed to take one thing at a time. Ingiborg wasn't blaming herself anymore, or at least not as much. Svanhilda was calming down.

Next on the agenda was the bear.

Kiúli took one more deep, centering breath, and opened his eyes to fix on the bear.

The bear clearly sensed its turn had come, for it sat up, locked gazes with the man, and spoke. "I'm sure you have many questions."

To his credit, Kiúli only blinked. He'd met talking creatures before—not many of them, but it *had* happened, and more than once. Truthfully, he'd somewhat suspected it—he'd never seen a bear with blue eyes before, and certainly never a bear that looked at Kiúli with such intelligence.

"A great deal, yes," Kiúli said, keeping his tone calm and conversational. "Most importantly, what happened to my daughter?"

At that, the bear shifted, looking distressed. "I do not know," he admitted. "She found the entrance to the vault, and somehow it let her inside, but she can't get out. Not even I can get her out."

Kiúli mulled that over. He had more questions, but he decided there was some more important information to gather first. "Who are you, to have so ready access to the vault?"

The bear bowed his head. As he did so, the light of the fire glinted off something around his neck, though he was far enough away and positioned so that Kiúli couldn't quite make it out. "I am Björn," the bear stated, his tone becoming formal, "and I am… the guardian of the vault, one might say." He sighed, ribcage heaving heavily, and his head drooped even lower. "And as guardian, it is my responsibility to protect the vault, and protect innocents from the powerful items that lie inside. I wasn't careful enough, it seems, and your daughter is paying for my mistakes. I am sorry."

There was a long moment of silence as Kiúli pondered this and

Björn stewed in his shame.

When Kiúli spoke, his words were slow and careful, his tone even. "As a father, it's my responsibility to be there for my children. I wasn't there to watch over her, and Rósfrída is stuck because of that. Do you think I'm to blame?"

Slowly, the bear raised his head, and shook it once.

Kiúli sighed, and as he did so, a faint smile, pained and bittersweet, pulled at his mouth. "Then I have no blame to lay upon you, either. You are only a bear, and I am only a man. Neither of us can be everywhere at once."

Björn's head lifted a little higher, and Kiúli could almost see the burden of guilt melting away. It wasn't completely gone—guilt was never vanquished so easily—but it was helped, and that would be enough.

Kiúli had long since learned it was better to reach for *enough* rather than *perfection*, for the latter was rarely, if ever, caught. And with the bear dealt with, there was only the most important thing left.

Slowly, carefully, Kiúli untangled himself from his girls, ushering them over to the nearest bed, helping Ingiborg lie down. She protested, at first, but her husband was firm.

"You need to rest your lungs," he said sternly, "and I've got a bit of a trip ahead of me."

Ingiborg looked at him as she pulled back her coverlet so Kiúli could coax Svanhilda into the bed beside her. Their eldest was nearly catatonic, shivering and shaking and half-blind from tears. It was a painful state for her parents—Svanhilda had always been the calm, collected child. This… this was unnatural, and it was rubbing salt in the wound left by Rósfrída's absence.

"You're going for help, aye?"

Kiúli tipped his head into a nod. "I'll be back soon, with a whole passel of your siblings. With thirteen of them, one of them should be able to figure it out."

There was a little beat of silence, and Ingiborg coughed, turning her attention to Svanhilda, who'd already fallen asleep. She was clearly exhausted, but her breath was uneasy, hitching now and again even in sleep. Calloused, careful fingers threaded through flaxen-pale locks. "And… and if they can't?"

Kiúli took a deep breath, let it out, repeated it. "It won't come to that," he said, keeping an iron grip on his voice and the hot, frantic feeling in his chest. If he gave into fear now, he'd be utterly useless. "And, even if it does, I shan't give up. There's got to be an answer somewhere." He picked up Ingiborg's hand and pressed it to his mouth, *hard*, and shut his eyes against the treacherous burn that lurked behind them. "And I swear to you, by the birds of the Wanderer and the very winds and waves of the Sea, that I won't rest until Rósfrída is home again."

A faint sob reached his ears, and the fingers in his hand trembled, though Kiúli didn't dare open his eyes to see if it was from fear or hope or some blend of the twain. He just needed to keep walking forward, and take it one thing at a time, and he'd figure it out.

He had to.

Unfortunately, it wasn't that simple.

Ingiborg had thirteen siblings—seven brothers and six sisters—and Kiúli brought all of them. Still, of them all, only two—Fáinn and Páiheid—had any knowledge of mirrors and suchlike, and even what they knew was little and insufficient. Even if they had known more, it swiftly became clear that Alvíss had carefully designed the vault to be safe from such tampering, so in the end their hands were tied. They kept trying, but as the sun rose on the fourth day of useless effort, they gave into the inevitable.

Kiúli, however, had made a promise, so he silently packed his bags, kissed his wife and daughter, and set off down the mountain.

"After all," he'd said to his wife, forced cheer ringing from his voice, "there are many strange and wonderful things in the world, things beyond our knowing and understanding, and there might yet be something out there that can help. And if there is, I'll find it."

Ingiborg clutched him tight, not wanting to say goodbye to yet another of her family, but in the end she stepped back. She stood in the threshold of her home, Svanhilda clinging to her hand just as fiercely as Ingiborg held hers, and they watched as Kiúli turned around the bend.

They weren't the only ones watching, however. Flosi was there, and had been for the past days, ever since a little girl slipped inside his wards and into a mirror.

"It's my fault, really," he muttered to himself, from his perch in a high pine. "I set the wards against those malicious and greedy, dangerous and suspicious, and never thought a threat might come from those who know nothing about the treasure." He laughed, a sound that would have been bright if it was not coated in bitterness and blame. "I should have known better."

This, of course, was not true. Flosi had no reason to suspect someone who didn't know anything about the vault to even be able to find it, hidden as it was. And even if they did, it would do them little good, for the vault was locked tightly and the key was hidden, and only Björn the Bear could come and go through the mirror-gate.

Unfortunately, Rósfrída was small and what power in her was weak and a mere echo of the maker of the mirror. So, when she had pressed against the glass, the mirror had been fooled, thinking Rósfrída herself was a part of it—a faint remnant of its master's power—and so she slipped through.

However, it is far easier to get *into* something than get *out* again. The mirror thought Rósfrída was a part of itself, and it would not suffer her to leave. She was well and truly stuck. Like a hand that reached into the tight mouth of a jar, Rósfrída could not withdraw, and there was no other way of escape—until a key could be found.

Even Flosi, for all his knowledge and skill, was not a dwarven smith. He could not control the mirror, nor bend it to his will, only subtly influence it… tweak a thread here or there.

And so, tweak a thread he did.

Rósfrída was a child of the wind and sea—Flosi knew this well. He was a bard, after all, and her soul fairly sang with the shush of waves and the whistle of the breeze. For such a child to be trapped, cooped up in a cage of stone and glass, was a travesty against the very nature of the world, and his blood boiled against it.

He could not fix it, but he could help. The only company she had was the bear, who would bring her food and clothes and do his best to look after her. Björn felt responsible, Flosi mused, but that was silly. It was clear where the blame lay.

While Björn tried his best, he was still a bear, and his best was only so much. But there was something more, something Flosi could work with.

An old promise, born from the faith of two children, strengthened by blood. *"We will not leave each other!"* and *"Never, never!"*

It was a small thing, but it was something; and a child's faith was a formidable "small thing", indeed. It was enough to build on.

Flosi settled his harp in his lap, lifting his fingers, and played a song of sisters.

There was a pretty song in Rósfrída's head, and she hummed loudly, trying to stave off the echoing the glass walls of her room seemed to love so much. At least it wasn't so quiet, since Björn was here now. When he was outside, the room was so empty, and there was only Rósfrída to fill it, and she was still quite small.

But when Björn was here, he sat down and let Rósfrída snuggle up against him, and he was delightfully warm and fluffy and chased away all the cold chill of the room. He wasn't only a good bear, the girl mused happily, but a great bear. And so nice and fluffy!

A sudden thought struck her, and Rósfrída perked up excitedly. She scrambled up from where she sat curled against the bear's side, and clambered up on top of Björn, perching on his shoulders and draping herself across his neck. "Mister Björn," she said thoughtfully, "Are we friends?"

The bear obediently held his head still, careful not to dislodge his tenant. "… I am not sure, little one, if I quite deserve to be your friend."

Rósfrída scowled. Well, that was silly. She didn't know why Mister Björn thought this, but it was clearly wrong. So, she decided to set him straight, and frowned fiercely. After a moment, she realized that, since she was on his back, he couldn't see her frown. Instead, she smacked him, hoping to communicate her displeasure. "That's silly, Mister Björn!"

"Oh?" the bear rumbled.

"Uh-*huh*!" she said firmly. "Don't you know? De-serv-ing has nothin' to do with being friends! All you have to do is want to, and I want to back!"

A sudden thought struck her, and she sucked in a breath, feeling her eyes prickle. She shrank down, trying to hide herself in Björn's thick fur. "Unless, 'course, you don't wanna be my friend."

The bear shook. It took a moment before Rósfrída realized he was laughing softly. It was a nice laugh, a little rumbly and huffy and growly, but it was warm and kind. "Nothing, little one, would be a greater honor than being your friend."

Rósfrída grinned as widely as if she'd been presented with *two* honeycombs to eat. She straightened, wrapping her arms as tightly about him as she could go. It wasn't a particularly impressive effort, but she'd done her best.

"Huzzah!"

She flopped on her back, staring up at the ceiling, which was, once again, a mirror. When she looked, however, she could see Svanhilda! The face was a bit rippled and wavy, which Rósfrída had learned meant the reflection was borne on water, but Rósfrída would know her big sister anywhere!

Rósfrída bit her lip and shrank against Björn's back. Björn, however, somehow sensed the twisting, sad emotions inside his charge and remained resolute, strong and warm at her back, and it gave her the courage to speak.

"Hi, Svana!" she chirped as cheerily as she could manage. "I wish you could hear me… and I could hear you. It's awful lonely, even if Mr. Björn *is* a good friend."

>>*<< · >>*<< · >>*<<

Svanhilda woke that morning with a song in her ears.

It was a lovely song, but strange—for she'd never heard it before, and yet it felt familiar as if she'd sung it all her life. She brushed it off, and set about her daily routine, trying to ignore the huge, aching gap left by the absence of a small red head darting about here and there like a bird on the wing. She passed her mother at the cookpot and frowned as she heard Ingiborg coughing slightly. If Svanhilda were Ingiborg's mother and not the other way round, Ingiborg would be resting in bed. Alas, Ingiborg *was* her mother, and she couldn't stand to lie in bed and think of her helplessness to save her youngest child.

So Svanhilda frowned and bit her tongue and prayed that Ingiborg would feel better. She silently got down the bucket and trotted outside to the stream. Her voice quietly hummed along with the song in her head, and she knelt at the water's edge, setting the bucket on the bank besides her. Quickly, the girl splashed water on her face to chase away the last of the sleepy wool in her head.

It didn't seem to quite work, for Svanhilda found herself staring at her uncertain, shadowed reflection on the stream's surface, as if entranced. Then—there was a shift in the current, a ripple on the surface of the water, and when it passed—

Svanhilda caught her breath in a gasp. She knew that face, perhaps even better than her own. But—but it wasn't possible—

"Hi, Svana!" said a voice Svanhilda would know anywhere. "I wish you could hear me... and I could hear you. It's awful lonely, even if Mr. Björn *is* a good friend."

Svanhilda wanted to gasp, or laugh, or cry, or all three at once. She couldn't quite manage that, however, so she went for the next best thing.

"Rósfrída!" she sobbed. "Rósfrída! I can hear you!"

"Do you see the mountain, Dagný?" Tryggvi said eagerly, looking down at his little sister nestled in his arms.

Queen Ljúfvina had, beyond all hope, conceived and born another child, two years after the first disappeared. Dagný, her father had named her—"new day"—and all the Folkbiörn loved her, and Tryggvi not the least. Indeed, to him she was his most precious thing, to be loved and cherished and protected.

He had had a great example of an older brother, after all, and he strived to put all of Ásbjörn's examples to good use.

The rest of his family saw Dagný as a gift from Highest Heaven to fill the empty, aching hole where a boy had once been. Tryggvi thought differently.

Not to put down his mother and father, but to him, Dagný was her *own* gift, and created a spot in his heart all her own, right next to a hole that Ásbjörn would one day fill for himself. He held his tongue about that thought, though, for he knew talk of his brother made his father and mother sad.

Instead, he brought Dagný out to the hill that arose above the town, cradled securely in his arms, and whispered to her stories about their big brother.

"Do you see it?" he said again, and Dagný stuck her thumb in her mouth, nodding shyly against his shoulder.

"I'm going to go there, soon as I'm old enough," he said confidently.

'And when exactly is that?' Allvaldi yawned from where he lay draped across one of Tryggvi's feet. Tryggvi ignored him in favor of his own bounding optimism, and continued without a missing a beat.

"And when I do, I'm gonna bring big brother Ásbjörn back home!"

Dagný lifted her head at this, eyes wide, though the thumb stayed firmly in place.

"Bovver A-born back?" she managed to say around her thumb, and Tryggvi nodded firmly.

"Yep! I'll bring him back, and he'll come home, and he'll give you a *big* hug."

Dagný considered this, sucking on her thumb solemnly. Finally, after a long silence, she spoke. "Pwomiss?"

Tryggvi grinned. "Promise. I'll bring him back, just wait and see."

It would be quite a bit of waiting and seeing, as Tryggvi was still only a boy, twelve winters old. But boys grow, given time, and become men.

And men keep their promises.

>>*<< · >>*<< · >>*<<

Seasons passed, and children grew until they were children no longer; yet little else changed and many things remained the same, on the mountain and in the Folkbiörn's town.

So the wide wheel of the year turned seven times.

PART 2

CHAPTER 1

"Are you gonna come back soon?"

Tryggvi looked down from where he was giving himself one last inspection, ensuring everything was ready for his journey. Dagný stared up at him, twisting one of her orange braids nervously and pressing herself tightly against Frode's side. Frode was an old fellow now, with a silvered muzzle and somewhat rheumy eyes, yet his bark was still loud and his legs still strong.

Tryggvi, like Frode, had been a constant presence by Dagný's side as she grew. And Tryggvi, having been raised knowing her eldest brother—the one whom she had never met, the one who had gone to the mountains and never returned—*well*. Tryggvi wasn't surprised she was apprehensive. So he crouched down in front of her, reaching out to give Frode a good scratch behind his ears.

"Yes," Tryggvi said. "I shan't be gone too long. All I have to do is find Ásbjörn first, and then I'll come right back so you can meet him." He lowered his voice and fished out the cord that hung around his throat, withdrawing the old, well-loved amber stone. "After all, I've got this."

Dagný's eyes grew wide, and she crept closer to give the stone a closer look. "What is it?"

"This," Tryggvi explained proudly, "is a gift my birth mother gave me a long time ago, and with it I can see all sorts of things I normally can't. Don't worry; with this, there's nothing that can keep our brother hidden from me." *Even if he looks different and smells odd, as Frode once said.*

"You don't use that stone to cheat at hide-an-seek, do you?" she accused, and Tryggvi laughed.

This caused her look to grow even more suspicious, so Tryggvi hastily swallowed his mirth and pulled on a sober mien. "I swear on the great white bear! I would never dishonor so great a game."

Dagný considered this, then jumped forward and slung her arms about Tryggvi's neck. Tryggvi, being a consummate older brother, was expecting this and caught her neatly with a laugh.

"I'll miss you," she whispered, and her brother smiled, squeezing her just a little bit tighter.

"And *I'll* miss *you,*" he whispered back. "Watch over old Frode for me while I'm gone?"

Dagný nodded firmly, and Tryggvi raised an eyebrow over her shoulder at the dog, who had sat down once he had no little mistress to support by standing. "The same goes for you, old fellow. I leave her in your care."

Frode let out a sharp bark, and Tryggvi smiled at the answer he received, well satisfied. His sister and his dog would look after one another. Not that he'd had any doubt, but it set his mind at ease to hear it out loud.

With that, he gave Dagný one last hug before standing up. Now there were only two farewells too bid.

King Ólaf and Queen Ljúfvina stood side by side, both looking solemn and weary. Tryggvi's heart panged within him, and he took in a deep breath, preparing himself.

Ljúfvina spoke first, clasping her hands together in front of her waist, her tone pleading. "Must you go?"

Tryggvi smiled, an expression somewhat bittersweet. "I must, Mother," he said calmly. "I have reason to believe he is there to be found; and as long as such reasons exist, I refuse to believe I hope in vain."

Ljúfvina nodded slowly, and Tryggvi turned to his father.

King Ólaf's expression was solemn, and he eyed his son up and down. "Are you sure you will not stay? I have great need of you here."

"You have plenty of retainers, Father, and I will not be gone long. Besides, I made a promise long ago, and you raised me to keep my word well. Would you have me do aught else?" Besides, Tryggvi knew that if he stayed much longer, King Ólaf would probably end up naming his remaining son his heir—and Tryggvi would not stand for that. That was Ásbjörn's place and Ásbjörn's throne, and while Tryggvi had been filling in during his brother's absence, to take it for his own was a betrayal of brotherhood that he would not stomach. Not without exhausting every other option first.

"No," Ólaf finally said heavily, but there was a faint twinkle in his eyes. "At least my one consolation is that you learned well."

His son replied with a short bow and a bright grin. "I ever aim to please, my king and father!"

"And you always hit your mark!" the King laughed back, before sobering. "But, if you cannot find him—"

"If I cannot find him after a year and day, then I will come home," Tryggvi vowed stoutly, "and take up whatever service of me you wish." Then he smiled, as bright and clear as the sun suddenly coming out from behind the clouds. "Don't worry, though—it won't come to that!"

So King Ólaf and Queen Ljúfvina gave him what benedictions they could offer, and Dagný gave Tryggvi a shy kiss on the brow, in imitation of their mother. Then Tryggvi shouldered his pack and strode away out the gate.

Some feet down the road, a shadow leapt out from the branch of a tree and landed heavily on Tryggvi's shoulder, claws digging in fiercely.

Tryggvi was used to this, however, and walked on without breaking his stride. His passenger was slightly miffed at this nonchalance but brushed it off with a wave of his fluffy golden tail.

'So, I take it you've got all those tedious goodbyes out of the way, and we can finally be on our way at last?'

"Tedious, hm?" Tryggvi laughed. "Says the one who was hiding in a tree so he wouldn't have to see my little sister cry that her fluffy cat friend is going with me."

'...you've gotten delusional in your dotage, I see.'

"Dotage?" A whoop of laughter rang out through the forest. "Ah yes, I see what you mean. I must have lost my wits, to think I could talk with cats."

Allvaldi had no response to this other than to dig his claws in a little deeper, but Tryggvi ignored them.

Tryggvi set his face to the North, where Alvíss' Mountain lay waiting.

>>*<< · >>*<< · >>*<<

The leaves were full and green with summer, the air beneath the branches shady and cool.

Tryggvi took a deep breath, running his fingers over the long, fluffy coat of the cat on his shoulder.

"Well, now, good master Allvaldi, where do you think we should start?"

The cat sniffed deeply, eyeing the forest around them. *'There's dwarf-power all over this place, down deep to the roots of the mountain. It'll be hard to distinguish anything, even for such a one as myself.'*

"Dwarf-power…" Tryggvi murmured. "But if it is truly so strong, why did it fail?"

'If there is no obvious gap in a strong gate, I would suspect the gate-keeper if an enemy sneaks through,' Allvaldi replied.

Tryggvi tilted his head to one side, eyes sweeping up and down the forest path, fingers skimming over the warm golden stone that hung about his neck. "Perhaps. But father assures me that the brothers Hánarr were and are trustworthy, or else they would not have been chosen for such a task."

'Well, since you have it all figured out, refrain from pestering me with useless questions,' Allvaldi replied, his whiskers bristling.

The lad smiled sheepishly and ran a finger over the back of Allvaldi's head, scratching gently at the crook of the neck. "Don't be so hasty, my friend! I was merely examining all the evidence. You have a fair point, indeed."

'Of course, I do,' Allvaldi sniffed. *'As if there was ever any doubt.'*

"I would never dare doubt you, my fine friend," Tryggvi said cheerfully, redoubling his scratching efforts at the base of Allvaldi's right ear. Allvaldi rumbled loudly, his chest thrumming strongly against Tryggvi's shoulder as he basked in his rightful due.

"Between your nose and advice, and my necklace…" Tryggvi

continued thoughtfully, as his free hand came up to let his fingers trail over the amber amulet dangling from a leather thong around his neck, "we'll figure out what happened, and we'll bring brother home.".

Well, if we want to figure out what's going on, might as well check out that spring over there. It's giving off some rather strange smells.'

"Strange smells?" Tryggvi immediately turned toward the spring.

'Indeed.' Allvaldi hopped down and landed gracefully on all four paws, then padded toward the edge of the spring cautiously to sniff. After a second, he stepped back, his whiskers shivering.

'It's as I thought,' the cat said. *'The water seems to be riddled with dwarf power, even more than the rest of this place. It's… odd. Normally, I wouldn't associate dwarves with water.'*

"Is it? Let me take a look and see what I can see," Tryggvi said, and trotted through the underbrush to the side of the spring, plopping down cross-legged and bending over the surface the water, his fingers going up to clutch at the piece of amber that hung from the cord around his neck. Holding it tightly, he peered deeply into the waters, eyes narrowed as he felt the cold stone slowly warm in his palm.

After a long moment, he blinked in surprise.

"Allvaldi, just to be sure—I haven't suddenly transformed into a girl with red hair, now have I?"

Allvaldi shot him a look, deeming the question below his dignity.

"As I thought," Tryggvi replied musingly. "Well, then that leaves us with another question. Why is my reflection a girl with red hair?"

Allvaldi blinked at him. Tryggvi stared back.

After a moment, Allvaldi shrugged, an elegant movement of sharp shoulder blades and excess fluff. *Why ask me? I'm simply a cat. I never have anything to do with water, if I can help it.'*

"Of course, 'simply a cat'. I find it amusing how you pull that card whenever it suits you best." Tryggvi raised an eyebrow, but his mouth was quirked with good humor.

Allvaldi was unperturbed, and set about smoothing his coat. *Why wouldn't I? As I said before, I am a cat, and while I may have loyalties, I answer to no one.'*

Tryggvi returned his gaze to the water, staring thoughtfully, tipping his head to one side to examine the reflection better, his fingers reaching out to touch the smooth surface of the water.

'I would be careful to avoid touching,' Allvaldi cautioned casually from where he sat. *'The water might be cursed, and the reflection it shows might be the ghost of some poor soul that drowned. You disturb the water, and you might end up cursed in turn.'*

Tryggvi jerked his hand back, his eyes wide with shock. "Do you think so?" he asked, his voice hushed.

'Not really.'

The man shot his companion a particularly dirty look. "Then why'd you say it?"

The cat flattened his ears and smirked. *'I'm a cat. As far as I'm concerned, all water is cursed.'*

Tryggvi rolled his eyes. "Ha. Very funny."

'Of course,' the cat replied. *'I am always funny.'*

"Yes, I've always thought you a veritable barrel of laughs," Tryggvi said, and returned his attention to the water and the reflection within.

Still, Allvaldi noticed the man made certain to avoid touching the surface of the water.

Tryggvi ran his fingers over the amber stone, his fingertips skimming over the long-familiar grooves and bumps on its surface, and he peered deeply into the water, trying to discern the source and truth of the image in the water.

It was a young woman, with a pale complexion and hair as red as the rowan berries that would ripen in the autumn. Her gaze, however, wasn't focused on him, but seemed to be gazing off into some distance that Tryggvi could not see. When he examined the reflection, however, there seemed to be a truth, a depth to the image, that he had never seen before in a mirror or the surface of a still pond.

Tryggvi propped his chin in his hand, eyeing the surface of the water curiously. He could speak to many things by the virtue of his mother's blood; he could hear the voices of bird and beast, listen to the songs of tree and brush and flower. Why couldn't he speak to a reflection?

It was worth a shot, at the very least. "Nothing ventured, nothing gained, after all," he said, then cleared his throat and called out loudly. "Excuse me, my lady? Can you hear me?"

The reflection's gaze snapped to meet his, and the girl's mouth dropped open.

"You can see me?" she squeaked.

Tryggvi grinned. "Since I'm talking to you, I would assume so."

The girl pouted, a rather adorable expression on her, and Tryggvi laughed ruefully in response. "I'm sorry, my lady. But it was an opportunity I couldn't resist. But yes."

"Your apology is accepted," she said primly. Her head tilted to one side. "But how can you see me? No one's ever able to see me from outside. Not even Björn. Only my sister can, but she's special."

Björn? Tryggvi's heart thumped, but he held back the sudden barrage of anxious questions that wanted to burst out of his mouth. "Ah, well, I'm not a particularly normal person, myself. But beyond that, I happen to have this." He withdrew his necklace over his head, and pinching the stone between his fingers, held it over the spring's surface. "It lets me see things that others cannot."

"Truly?" the girl said, her eyes wide. "It doesn't seem like dwarf-make. It's just a stone."

"It *isn't* dwarf-make, true… I don't rightly know where it's from, only that it's from far away and is very special," Tryggvi explained. "But as long as I touch it, I can see you."

"Well, I wish more people had fancy stones like that," the girl said with a sigh. "It's very boring, to see everything and to have almost no one see you in return."

"I would imagine so."

'Almost as bad as being able to hear everyone but have no one hear you,' Allvaldi sighed sympathetically. He prowled closer, staying well away from the water's edge, but close enough to dig his claws into Tryggvi's cloak and tug. *'Tell the girl I sympathize with her plight.'*

Tryggvi rolled his eyes. "My cat wants you to know that he shares your pain, as he has lots of things to tell humans and they cannot hear him. Whether *that* is a blessing or curse, I shall keep my own counsel."

The reflection girl laughed. "You have a talking animal friend, too?"

Tryggvi cocked an eyebrow at that—*too* was an interesting word to use—but replied, "No, nothing so grand."

Allvaldi dug his claws in a little deeper to convey what exactly he felt about *that* statement, but Tryggvi ignored him, well-used to the cat clawing at his clothes.

"My cat *is* a forest cat, and of the kind blessed by the Powers, but I can understand him because of the virtue of my mother's blood. She was of the elven kin, and the words of the beasts that dwell in the forest are clear to my ears."

"Elven blood? How wonderful!" The reflection clapped her hands excitedly, her eyes wide. "I have dwarven blood, myself. I never thought I'd meet someone else like me."

"The world is full of strange and wonderful things!" Tryggvi laughed.

The reflection girl did not. Instead, her face became downcast. "I wouldn't know. I haven't been outside this room for years."

Tryggvi straightened slowly, his brow furrowing. "What do you mean?"

The girl laughed sheepishly, looking away. "Ah, well… when I was a little girl I found a strange mirror, and it trapped me inside a room, and I haven't been able to get out."

Tryggvi stared solemnly down at the reflection. She was clearly a little girl no longer—a young woman, only a year or two younger than himself, at most.

"That's… a long time to be stuck in one room," he said, his voice quiet.

"Ah, well, it's not *too* bad!" she replied, forcing cheer into her voice and smiling. It was a fragile smile, however, and Tryggvi didn't need his amber stone to see the truth it hid.

His heart ached. And in that moment, a decision was made, an ambition set.

He hoped Mother wouldn't be too mad at him if his return was a little delayed, because he had no plans to leave this mountain until this girl was free.

"After all," the girl continued hastily, "my sister can see me, so we can still talk, and if I hadn't gotten stuck in here, I probably would have never met Björn!"

Björn! There was that name again. Hope and fear blended together within him, an anxious heat rising in his chest. "And who is Björn?"

The girl brightened, and the fragility of her smile vanished, bolstered by her honest delight, and some of the ache in Tryggvi's heart was eased. "Björn is my friend! He's the one who's kept me alive all this time—*he* can leave my room, so he goes and gets food and clothes for me from my family and brings them back! I don't know what I'd do without him."

Tryggvi, however, frowned. "If this Björn can come and go as he pleases from your room, why hasn't he helped you get out yourself?"

If this man was taking advantage of this poor girl, *well*—Tryggvi would just have to introduce him to the error of his ways.

But then the girl laughed. "Don't be silly; Björn is a bear! How is he supposed to be able to help me?"

…A *bear?* "Oh! Your talking animal friend."

She nodded, smiling fondly. "He may be only a bear, but he's a good bear, and a very great friend. My sister thinks so, too!"

"I'm glad you have a friend, then." Tryggvi smiled and reached over and laid his hand on Allvaldi's back. "When you're lonely, a friend makes all the difference."

Allvaldi purred and leaned into the touch, and Tryggvi's smile grew.

The girl, however, merely tilted her head to one side, eyeing him curiously. "You sound like you know the feeling. What was your prison?"

Tryggvi's gaze shot up to meet hers, one eyebrow raised. "Why do you think I had a prison?"

"I live in a mirror," she replied, "and aren't mirrors supposed to reflect what they see? I'm just doing what I'm supposed to. And… and your words and your eyes are like those of someone who knows what it is to be trapped."

The man laughed, leaning his cheek on a fist. "You're a strange girl," he said, "but yes, I suppose you could say I've been trapped. I have a brother who went missing long ago, and I wasn't able to go out and look for him ere now."

The girl sighed. "That sounds like my sister. She tries to hide it, but I know her. I can tell she's lonely."

"Loneliness and helplessness," Tryggvi said, his voice deep and sad, "are a special prison of their own. I am sorry for your sister, and I hope she can be reunited with you soon."

The girl blinked, then furiously wiped at her eyes with her sleeve. When the last of the dampness had been chased away, she bowed her head with gratitude. "That means a lot. And I wish you luck in finding your brother!"

She smiled, and he bowed his head in return. Before the conversation could continue, however, Allvaldi decided they had risked enough time near the body of water ('*Water is treacherous, after all—what if it suddenly became alive and attacked them? What then?*'). So, he rammed his claws into Tryggvi's thigh and made a particularly loud, wordless complaint.

Tryggvi knew well that there was no changing the cat's mind when he got in such moods, so he turned back to the reflection. "Well, my lady, my cat is demanding that we be off, so I am afraid I'll have to take my leave of you."

She looked a little disappointed, but she quickly waved it off, smiling brightly. "Of course! I am glad to have met you and made a new friend."

"We can hardly be friends if we don't know each other's name," Tryggvi replied casually. "Let's fix that, shall we?"

He slid into a smooth bow, letting his twin braids hang heavily towards the ground. "I am Tryggvi Brandr Ólafsson, at your service."

By going first, he hoped to ease any apprehensions she might have, and it seemed to do the trick, for she answered him quite cheerfully. "Rósfrída Ingiborgardottir, at your's and your family's."

With that done and out of the way, Rósfrída beamed eagerly. "Now that we are friends, if you ever feel the need to ask me something, just look into a mirrored surface or reflection and call my name! I'll be able to see you then."

"I don't carry a mirror," Tryggvi hummed thoughtfully, mentally going through the contents of his pack. "My dagger is quite sharp and polished to a mirror shine; will that work?"

"That will work just fine!" Rósfrída bounced up and down in excitement. "It'll be nice to have someone new to talk to!"

"I could say the same," Tryggvi said warmly. "It'll be good to have someone along who isn't completely full of himself."

Rósfrída burst out into laughter, while Allvaldi casually cleaned a particularly finicky spot on his right leg. Once that was complete, he finally decided to deign Tryggvi's remark with his attention.

'I am merely being what I was born to be; that is, a cat. If you want a lackey of a lapdog to inflate your fragile human ego, then be my guest." He stood up and stretched, while Tryggvi simply watched him in amusement. *'I'll return home to the comforts your sister shall lavish upon me.'*

With a magnificent flick of his fluffy tail, Allvaldi turned his back on man and stream and began to trot away. *'Good luck finding your brother without my nose.'*

He had managed to take a grand total of five steps when hands suddenly closed around his abdomen, snatching him up into the air. Allvaldi exploded into a tiny, hissing whirlwind of claws and golden fur.

'PUT ME DOWN, YOU INSOLENT WRETCH—'

"Now, now, Master Allvaldi, you know I appreciate you greatly—"

'VENGEANCE, I TELL YOU. YOU WON'T GET AWAY WITH THIS! VENGEANCE WILL BE MINE!'

Tryggvi merely held the cat at arm's length, not even phased by the fluffy ball of fury incarnate within his grasp.

Truly, experience is a wonderful thing.

"So, Rósfrída, tell me—" Tryggvi asked, holding his dagger out and at his side, so he needed to merely glance down to see the mirror-girl. "What kind of mirror is it, exactly, that you got stuck in?"

Rósfrída frowned, eyes narrowing suspiciously. "Why do you want to know?"

"Well, it's not like most mirrors go around trapping people inside them, you know," he replied, his voice calm. Clearly, the mirror was a sensitive subject.

Be that as it may, however, he needed to find out as much as he could about it. Knowledge was power, after all, and if he wanted to free Rósfrída, he'd need all of both that he could get.

"True…" Rósfrída considered. "Very well, I'll tell you—as long as you *promise* not to try and get in for yourself!"

Tryggvi hummed thoughtfully. "I promise not to use what you tell me for my own gain."

He didn't know much about mirrors, though he'd heard some dark, frightening rumors over the years about what could happen if a powerful mirror fell into the hands of someone black of heart. From what he knew of mirrors in general and *this* one in particular, they seemed dangerous; and that kind of danger was not something the wise man challenged heedlessly. His only interest in the mirror was how to get Rósfrída *out* of it.

"Very well," Rósfrída said, nodding in satisfaction. "Hmm… how do I explain this?"

"The beginning is usually a good place to start," Tryggvi supplied, and she smiled at him.

"Well, then, the beginning is that I had a grandfather once; his name was Alvíss the Smith, and he was known all over for his skills!"

There was a long moment of silence, stretching out as slowly as honey. "… Alvíss the Smith." Tryggvi's voice was faintly downcast, and Rósfrída fluttered a little in concern, wondering what she could do to help soothe his spirits.

"I've heard of him, before," Tryggvi said at length, raising his head, shoulders back and thoughtful smile on his face, as if his long moments of silence had never happened. "He's known for making many great and wondrous things."

"That's Grandfather all right!" She cocked her head and straightened her shoulders with pride. "And the *King himself* commissioned him to create an extra special vault for the kingdom's most valuable treasures." Her enthusiasm petered out slightly. "And he did it—he created a vault inside a mirror. And then… and then Grandfather and Great-Uncle died, and no one knows how to work the vault anymore.

"And then, well… then I got stuck. And no one could get me out."

"No one?" Tryggvi asked curiously.

"Yes, no one! A great many people tried! All of Mama's brothers and sisters, and some wise men and dwarves they knew. Papa keeps going on voyage after voyage trying to find a way to help, but nothing's worked."

Well. It seemed it'd be a bit more difficult than he anticipated, but he honestly should have expected that. Still, difficulties or not, it didn't matter. He'd made up his mind, and he wouldn't let something so small as 'no one's managed it before' stop him.

Then what Rósfrída had said trickled through his mind, and he froze mid-step. The story sounded awfully familiar… What was it?

"So how many brothers and sisters does your mother have?" Tryggvi asked semi-absently, as he tried to dig through the annals of his mind and find what bell had just been rung.

"Oh!" Rósfrída exclaimed, flustered. She held up her hands and frowned down at her fingers, brows furrowing as she thought hard.

Tryggvi smiled at the look of concentration on her face; it was a rather adorable view.

"Well, first there's Uncle Fáinn, he's the oldest. Then Uncles Úri and Thekkr, that's three," she said, ticking down her fingers as she went. "Then Aunt Ásgerda and Aunt Reidunn, then Uncle Kili—his name is funny 'cause it sounds like Papa's; then there's Uncle Glói and Aunt Vífrid and Aunt Halldóra; then Uncle Nefir. Then there's Ingiborg, that's my mother. Then after Mama, it's Aunt Jardís and Uncle Ívaldi, and last of all its Aunt Páiheid! And that's all of them. So… Mama has thirteen siblings in all—the fourteen Alvíssung."

Ah! And there it was.

Tryggvi lay on his stomach on the bearskin draped in front of the hearth, legs kicking up and down idly as he teased Allvaldi with a piece of string. Frode was curled up against his side, sides heaving up and down slowly in contentment. Father was carving arrows, and mother was winding yarn, preparing it to be dyed.

"Father, that dwarf Björn is studying with—how come he has a whole mountain? And nearby, too? I thought most dwarves lived further north, where the mountains are thicker."

"Aye, that's true," Ólaf rumbled, setting down his knife. "Master Alvíss came to us when your grandfather was king and I was still a lad, many years ago now, asking for permission to take a nearby mountain as his own. My father

agreed, on the condition that Master Alvíss agreed to make a special vault for our family's most valuable and powerful heirlooms and treasures, and hide it on that mountain where they'd be nearby, but safe."

"Valuable and powerful things?" Tryggvi asked, intrigued enough to roll onto his back so he could sit up, luring Allvaldi into his lap with tempting flicks of the string. "Like what?"

"Oh, there's too many to describe in one sitting, my son," his father laughed. "After all, our family has a long history of adventures. It's no surprise we've gathered quite a lot of interesting heirlooms."

"Then tell me about one!" Tryggvi bounced a little, trying to contain his excitement. "Please? Pleasepleaseplease?"

Ólaf laughed again, and settled back in his chair, picking up the knife and beginning to work on another arrow shaft as he thought. "Well, my personal favorite is Farbiörn's pelt. Farbiörn Bjarnhedin, you know, was our first ancestor, and a very great man. A wise leader and powerful warrior. One day, however, he got trapped into a deal with an untrustworthy Power—and might have met a terrible end."

Tryggvi gasped, and Ólaf smiled into his beard. "However, the Wanderer found him, and in his kindness and mercy gave to Farbiörn a mighty gift: the pelt of a great white bear, which, when put on, would turn the wearer into such a creature. That is how he came to be known as Bjarnhedin, and we his descendants as the Björning, and our people the Folkbiörn. The bear, especially the great white bear, has become our symbol. The pelt of Bjarnhedin was cherished for a great many years as an heirloom of our house, until one day it came into the hands of an evil woman, who used it to curse her step-son, Prince Býulfr—but I'm sure that story is one you're well familiar with."

"That's where Prince Býulfr's pelt came from?" Tryggvi gasped. "I had no idea!"

"The pelt has a long story behind it indeed," Ólaf said solemnly, "and it has touched the stories of many others; though of its origin, only the Wanderer himself can tell."

Tryggvi leaned back on one arm, using his free hand to absently rub up and down his kitten's back. "That sounds really amazing," he said. "I'd like to see this pelt one day! And maybe put it on!"

His father laughed indulgently and leaned forward to ruffle Tryggvi's hair. "Well, in a few years you'll be off to study under Master Alvíss, and you can try it on for yourself."

"I don't want to wait a couple years, though!" Tryggvi protested. *"I bet Ásbjörn's trying it on all the time without me."*

"Maybe so, but there must be some privileges along with the burdens of being eldest," his father said, and ruffled Tryggvi's hair again. *"But there are just as many privileges that come with being the youngest, so you'll just have to bear it."*

Well.

So Rósfrída was trapped in the special vault created by Master Alvíss for his family. That certainly made things interesting. If the vault was as secure as Alvíss had promised, and Alvíss had died before he could tell anyone else the secrets to opening it, no wonder Rósfrída was trapped. How she got in was another mystery, but it might have had something to do with being the master craftsman's granddaughter.

No matter: all it meant was the puzzle would be even more interesting to unravel than he'd anticipated.

The memory had sparked another thought inside Tryggvi's mind, one that made his heart skitter in anticipation.

"Tell me, Rósfrída," he said, slowly, "how familiar are you with the contents of that vault?"

She snorted, lifting her chin proudly. "What do you think? It's been seven years since I crossed into the mirror; I know every single item like the back of my hand."

"Then," Tryggvi asked, taking a deep breath, and trying to calm his heart like he would a skittish horse, "have you ever seen the pelt of a great white bear amongst the other treasure?"

"A white bear's pelt?" She tilted her head to one side thoughtfully. "I can't say I have… there's plenty of pelts and furs in here, but not one like that. The only white bear I know is Björn, but he's very much alive and in possession of his fur!"

Tryggvi's lungs constricted, somehow caught halfway between a sigh of relief and a gasp.

It wasn't proof, not by a long shot—but it was a possibility.

And after ten long years of no word and stubborn hope built on small things, it was enough to make his head swim like he'd just taken a swig of an aged mead. His hope had *not* been in vain, just as he'd always believed, and what he searched for might be just within the reach of his hands.

"But—" Rósfrída said sharply, "why are you asking? You said you had no interest in what lies inside the mirror."

Well, that wasn't entirely true. Tryggvi was finding himself more and more interested in one particular denizen of the mirror; but that wasn't what Rósfrída had meant.

"I'm not interested in the way you're thinking—I've heard enough stories about powerful mirrors to steer well away," Tryggvi said, holding up his free hand. "I just have a suspicion that the bear pelt I mentioned had something to do with my brother's disappearance, and I knew it used to be contained in that vault."

Rósfrída narrowed her eyes at him, refusing to budge just yet. Björn was the guardian of the vault, and he'd been so kind to her, not to mention that the vault had been in Grandfather's keeping. It was her duty to protect it, even from someone as nice as Tryggvi seemed to be.

"How do you know that? How come you're familiar with the insides of the vault?"

"Because," Tryggvi said seriously, "my father's father commissioned the vault, and the heirlooms of my house are held inside."

There was a long moment of silence. Rósfrída blinked. When she finally spoke again, her voice had risen an octave or two. "*Your* father's father?"

"Yes, my Grandfather Thjalfi," Tryggvi replied, taking perhaps just a bit too much amusement from the situation.

"Then…" she said, her voice still squeaking. Tryggvi thought It rather cute, like a disgruntled rabbit. "When you said your name was Tryggvi Ólafsson, you mean your father was *King* Ólaf?"

Tryggvi bowed his head. "Indeed, I did. I am Tryggvi Brandr of the Björning, at your service."

When he lifted his head again, Rósfrída was still staring, her face as red as her hair. At the sight of his face, her hands flew up to cover her embarrassment, mumbling incoherent apologies into her palms.

Tryggvi simply smiled calmly, though she couldn't see. "Please, you don't need to apologize! You did nothing wrong, and I'm not mad."

At his assurance, she peeked over her fingers. Seeing from his expression that he truly wasn't mad, her hunched shoulders relaxed, and her hands dropped. Tryggvi brightened his smile, hoping to put her at ease. "After all, Ólaf is a common name. It'd be rather silly to assume every Ólafsson you meet is the son of a King."

"Exactly!" Rósfrída huffed self-righteously, confidence regained and sparkling with mischief. "So you shouldn't tease poor, innocent ladies like myself!"

"Very true," Tryggvi said solemnly, and bowed his head again to hide the answering twinkle in his eyes. "I offer my humble apologies, my lady. I can only hope you will forgive me."

"Oh, well… I suppose," she said, then burst into laughter. It was a lovely sound, bright and cheerful, every note a victory over her circumstances, and it made Tryggvi's heart beat just a little bit faster.

So he started laughing with her, bursting full with the happiness of answers within reach, and good company, and a bright summer day.

Allvaldi, who was trotting slightly behind his companion, stopped and rolled golden eyes towards the heavens.

'I can see where this is going. Lovely,' he groaned. *'Just lovely.'*

He might have continued to make several pointed comments, not being a particular believer in maxims concerning brevity and wit, but instead he froze. A delicate pink nose lifted to the wind, sniffing deeply, before darting forward and batting at Tryggvi's leg.

'Tryggvi! Stop that infernal racket and follow me!'

Without even waiting for the man, the cat darted off to one side, racing uphill through the pinewood. Tryggvi blinked after him in astonishment, then glanced down at the blade of his knife.

"I have to go now, sorry!" He frowned. "Something's gotten into Allvaldi."

"O-oh!" Rósfrída blinked, her expression falling somewhat. "Of course! Stay safe and best of luck…" She took a deep breath, then pushed it out, smiling as brightly as she could. "Until later?"

Her voice was full of hope and cheer, but he could see behind the veneer to the uncertainty it tried to hide.

So he smiled, full of warmth and compassion, trying to push every ounce of his sincerity into his voice. "Until then, Rósfrída."

He only caught a glimpse of the brilliance of her smile and shining eyes before he sheathed his dagger and took off through the woods after Allvaldi, but it caused a warmth to fill his chest until he felt it could burst.

He pushed that aside though—whatever it was that the cat had smelled, it was clearly important, and Tryggvi couldn't afford to be distracted—pleasant though the distraction may be.

It was only a minute before he caught sight of a spot of gold at the base of a tree up ahead, and Tryggvi ran up to him at full speed, skidding to a stop at the last second. The cat didn't even look up to acknowledge his arrival, though that wasn't particularly out of the ordinary. Tryggvi instead crouched down to be closer to Allvaldi's level and lowered his voice.

"What is it? Did you smell something?"

'*Oh, I smelled something, all right,*' the cat drawled, and with a flick of his tail, pointed with his nose towards the left. '*Take a look for yourself.*'

Tryggvi did.

He gasped.

There, some thirty feet away, a white bear was walking through the woods.

Or, at least to Allvaldi's eyes it appeared to be a white bear.

To Tryggvi, who had a certain amber stone lying against the skin of his chest, he saw a large bear with fur as white as snow—but at the same time, he saw a tall man with pale hair, blue eyes, and a familiar face.

He sat down, hard, with wide eyes and shallow, hasty breaths.

It is one thing to guess, to hypothesize, to hope—it is quite another to see it to be true.

Tryggvi buried his face in his hands and sobbed.

Despite all the years that had passed, and his clinging, persistent fear… he hadn't forgotten the face of his brother.

>>*<< · >>*<< · >>*<<

"You're saying…" Rósfrída said slowly, "that my friend Björn is your long-lost brother under a curse?"

Tryggvi nodded once, lips tight. He was sitting at the base of that same pine tree, leaning against the wood, ignoring the stickiness the pine resin would doubtlessly leave on his clothes and hair. He hardly felt like his legs would hold him up right now. Allvaldi had declared Tryggvi's lap as his rightful conquest, and Tryggvi was holding the dagger so he could look at Rósfrída as he explained the situation. It had taken a bit of time—he'd ended up telling her how exactly he'd been adopted into the clan of the Björnings. By now, the sun was low in the sky, sending golden shafts of light filtering through the pine branches to lay across the forest floor, paired with impossibly long shadows stretching across the ground.

"And you're absolutely certain?" she asked, arching an eyebrow. She wasn't *exactly* skeptical, but it was a little hard to believe. After all, she'd known Björn for seven years, and she'd only met Tryggvi that day.

"Positive." Tryggvi swallowed hard, licking his dry lips. "The stone that enables me to see you shows me the truth of things. Whatever curse it is that lies on Björn, it cannot change the fact that beneath that fur, he *is* a man."

"Hm." Rósfrída crossed her arms and furrowed her brow, thinking hard. "Well… if he *is* a man, I suppose that would explain a few things." She glanced up, a sad frown pulling at her lips. "Then… that means, this whole time he's been helping me, he's been cursed, too."

Tryggvi nodded, again, his chest and throat too tight to speak. Allvaldi rubbed his chin against Tryggvi's knee, purring loudly. Tryggvi's muscles began to slowly relax, and his free hand found its way into Allvaldi's thick, soft fur. The purring redoubled.

Rósfrída hummed again, and then a look of determination crossed her face, her eyes blazing as fiercely as a shieldmaiden's. "Right! That just means I'll have to do everything I can to help you help him! I owe him an awful lot, you know."

"Truly?" Tryggvi said, a faint smile crossing his face.

Rósfrída nodded firmly. "Truly! He's my best friend, and he's been helping my family take care of me, and keeps me company. So it's about time I got a chance to return the favor."

"Then, do you have any ideas on how to help him?" Tryggvi asked hopefully.

The girl flushed, tugging at one of her braids and looking off to one side. "Well… uh, since I never really noticed Björn wasn't actually a bear before… um, not really."

Tryggvi flushed in turn, his free hand darting to rub sheepishly at the back of his neck. Allvaldi's purring stuttered to an abrupt stop, and the cat lifted his head to send a particularly nasty glare at the sudden lack of his rightful due. "Oh, right. I… I hadn't thought of that."

All three fell silent, minds furiously racking themselves for some sort of idea or plan—at least, that was the origin of Rósfrída's and Tryggvi's silence. Allvaldi's brand was rather more petulant and offended.

Tryggvi bit his lip, tugging out his charm and rolling the amber stone back and forth between his thumb and forefinger.

"Wait…" Rósfrída suddenly said, her eyes widening, "I might—"

"Funi, well met! I'd set out to find you, but I didn't think it would be so soon!" Another voice cut in, loud, somewhere between jovial and bemused, and very strange in sound. "Whatever are you doing here at this time of the year? No matter, I need to talk to you about that family of yours. I have no idea what's going on, but *something* definitely is. It's even starting to affect us, so *clearly* it's something significant. Father's starting to worry about the integrity of the harvests if this continues—"

A tall figure, silhouetted and limned in gold by the late afternoon, stepped out from behind the trunk of a large old pine tree. The next second, the figure froze, and when he spoke his tone was still jovial, but sharper than a thicket of spears.

Allvaldi leapt to his feet in Tryggvi's lap, tail and fur puffing up and a snarl pulling at his lips.

Tryggvi himself could not move—partly because of the frightened cat in his lap, but mostly because he had the distinct impression if he even twitched in the wrong direction, he'd be sliced to ribbons.

"Well, well, what do we have here?" the man said, folding his arms and glaring down at Tryggvi and his cat. "Tell me, who are you, and why you smell like my friend—and I might not strike you down on the spot."

CHAPTER 2

There was a shuffling sound at the door, and Svanhilda looked up from her carding with a smile.

"That sounds like Björn," Ingiborg said fondly, smiling as she passed her shuttle through the warp threads on her loom. "Go and see what he wants and be sure to bring the satchel of supplies for Rósfrída."

Svanhilda, however, paused as she was setting aside her carding combs. "Are you sure I should go, Mother? Are you feeling well enough?"

Ingiborg scoffed, waving a hand. "I feel just fine. I'm not so far along that I need to be watched, and the little one has been giving me no trouble. My breath and lungs are fine. Go on and have a nice walk with our friend and give Rósfrída my love."

Svanhilda still frowned, so Ingiborg turned and smiled with a sigh, gesturing for her daughter to go ahead. "Go *on!* And while you're out, why don't you pick some mint for me?"

Svanhilda's frown increased, biting her lip. "If you are feeling ill enough to want mint—"

"Then it simply means I want mint for my stomach," Ingiborg said firmly. "If you are so worried, then go and fetch some for me, darling."

Svanhilda sighed, and then smiled, and put away her tools and the wool she was working with. She fetched the satchel and kissed her mother's cheek, then left the house.

Björn was sitting by the stream that ran not far from the house, eyeing the fish that darted down the currents hungrily. When he heard the door closing, however, he lifted his head and clambered to his feet.

"Good afternoon, Svanhilda," the bear rumbled politely. "And how have you been on this fine summer's day?"

Svanhilda felt a smile spreading across her face, and she ran over to meet him, flinging her arms as much as she could around his neck. Björn chuckled good-naturedly and nuzzled his nose against the back of her head.

After a couple seconds, she stepped back, still smiling brightly as she adjusted her satchel over her shoulder. "I've been quite well, thank you," she said. "How are you, and Rósfrída?"

"Besides rather hungry, I am quite well," Björn said, sending a hopeful gaze toward the woman beside him.

Svanhilda rolled her eyes, though it didn't detract from her smile as she reached into the satchel and dug out a piece of dried cod, tossing it into the air. Without missing a beat, Björn snatched it out of the air and swallowed it back, rumbling his delight.

The woman beside him sighed happily and clasped her hands behind her back, beginning to stroll in the direction of Björn's cave. Björn matched her walk, still licking his chops contentedly. Finally, after the last of the taste had been absorbed, he spoke. "But why ask me about little Rósfrída? You speak with her far more often than I."

"Yes…" Svanhilda twisted the string of beads that hung between her broaches, frowning. "But she's been unusually distracted today." She reached into one of the pouches that hung from her belt and withdrew the mirror that her father had gifted her all those years ago, after she'd first discovered Rósfrída in her reflection.

She could see Rósfrída there even now—but her face was turned away, Svanhilda's gaze meeting the back of her little sister's red head. "I just wonder what has so much of her attention."

Björn paused, lifting his head thoughtfully. "I've caught a new smell on the wind several times today—and on the way to your house, I heard someone laugh. There's someone else on the mountain."

Svanhilda stopped and turned to face him, clasping her hands nervously in front of her stomach. "Really? You're certain it's not that elf you've noticed hanging around? Even I've heard him laugh once or twice."

The bear shook his head. "No, I am mostly certain this was a different voice. And the scent—I am nearly certain it was a man."

Svanhilda bit her lip, considering this. "If it's a man… do you think it could be someone from your family, come to look for you?"

Björn turned his head away. "I doubt it," he said. "I closed that chapter of my life a long time ago. He has forgotten me by now, as he should."

"With all due respect, Master Björn," Svanhilda replied solemnly, "if he is your brother, and loves you even a fraction of the amount I love *my* sister, he could never forget you."

It hadn't taken Svanhilda very long to suspect there was more to the bear she and her sister had befriended than met the eye. He hadn't *acted* very much like a bear and he had seemed rather knowledgeable about the habits of men. And his eyes were that strange shade of blue. Still, everyone knew talking beasts were mysterious creatures, so she'd brushed it off for a while, and might have dismissed it entirely… if it hadn't been for the torque.

She slanted her eyes to one side, eyeing the torque even now.

Of Ingiborg's children, Svanhilda was the one whose blood ran truest toward the folk of the mountains. Rósfrída was often insensate of the rhythms of the power of the dwarves, and had to focus intently to pick anything out, but Svanhilda was not so hindered.

She could *feel* the dwarf-power in the silver torque around his neck—but it was odd. It wasn't embedded in the torque in a natural manner; the power wasn't something that had been added carefully as the metal was shaped and pounded and formed.

No, it had been added later, and hastily, and—it felt sick. Wrong, and cruel, and choking.

Svanhilda had only brought it up to her mother once. Ingiborg's face had paled, and she had held Svanhilda close as her eyes darkened with sorrow.

"Whatever power lies on that thing—it is beyond my knowing, and beyond the knowing of all my siblings. It's dark, and I lack the ability to shine light on it. I cannot help the one who has helped us so much."

So Svanhilda did not bring it up again. But she watched the bear carefully, and carefully put the pieces she held together: the strange torque, Björn's mannerisms, the legends of the Björnings, who could take on the shape of a white bear—such as the tale of Prince Býulfr, one of Rósfrída's favorite bedtime stories… and once, she had heard Grandfather tell her father he had taken on a student—the prince of the Folkbiörn—shortly before the accident had happened.

One day, when the rain poured down from the heavens and Björn sat drying his wet hide in front of their fire—just like that first day a year before—Svanhilda had spoken into the silence left by her slumbering parents.

"You're a boy, aren't you. Not a bear. Not really," she had said, and Björn had lifted his head from his paws, staring at her solemnly.

"Yes."

His voice was quiet, his eyes shadowed. Svanhilda had sighed, then shuffled over across the straw of the floor to lean against his side.

"Why didn't you say anything?"

"I can't, not by myself." He shook his head once, and the silver torque gleamed strangely in the firelight as it shifted. "The lock on me insists that I cannot speak of it, not unless the one I'm addressing brings it up first."

The girl nodded solemnly, even though he couldn't see it. "I wondered if it was something like that. Then, do you want me to tell Rósfrída?"

There was a long silence, before finally he shook his head once. Svanhilda sighed again. She understood why, or at least she was pretty sure she did, but she still thought it wasn't the best choice.

But it was his choice to make.

Svanhilda sighed for the third time—it was an evening for sighs, apparently, and nestled in closer against his side, heedless of the faint dampness to his fur.

"I wish I could help." Her voice was quiet, murmured, but he'd heard it clearly all the same.

He sighed deeply, his sides heaving once. "I thank you, but there is nothing to be done."

"Are you certain?" she'd pressed. "Can you tell me who did this? If I knew that, maybe I could make them stop."

"No, I can't tell you," Björn replied, and Svanhilda frowned. She'd expected as much, but it still was vexing to hear.

"But even if I could, I would not tell you," he said, and Svanhilda startled at the firmness, the fierceness in his voice. "I refuse to place such a burden upon you. I will not let it be; such a thing is not something that you should ever bear."

She stared at him in wonder, and had long pondered what he had meant, and what secrets lay behind his words.

She was still wondering even now, six years later.

They reached Björn's cave a little while later, Svanhilda carefully edging along the path and ducking behind the waterfall. Björn simply swam right underneath it and hauled himself up into the cave on the other side, then shook himself like a dog. Svanhilda, who had made this trip many, many times, managed to dart out of the way of the far-flung drops just in time.

Like every other time, she sent the bear a look of utmost disapproval. He merely returned it with a bear's best approximation of a grin.

With a roll of her eyes, Svanhilda turned to the mirror inlaid on the wall, and observed her reflection.

Here, at this mirror, was the only spot Svanhilda could get a good look at her little sister. Rósfrída had shot up like a weed and was almost as tall as Svanhilda now—a deep injustice indeed! Her legs and arms were spindly, though, and her skin had changed as well. What had once been freckled and slightly ruddy from all her days spent in the sun, was now pale and wan, starved of light and warmth.

It never failed to make something deep in Svanhilda's gut twinge with guilt, but she kicked it away, just as she always did. Rósfrída had told her long ago that she didn't blame Svanhilda at all, and Svanhilda knew no good came from dwelling on the mistakes of the past. That only led to regrets, and regrets were a heavy chain indeed.

But now, just as before, Rósfrída was turned away from her sister, and that made a different something twinge inside. Just *what* was going on?

"Rósfrída, are you listening?"

Rósfrída jumped, and she spun around, eyes wide, only to relax when she realized who stood in front of her mirror. Her smile widened, and she spread her arms wide in her best attempt at a hug. "Svana! It's good to see you!"

Despite herself, Svanhilda softened, and smiled. "It's good to see you too, Rósfrída."

They smiled at each other for several seconds before Svanhilda spoke, still smiling sweetly. "So, what has you so distracted today?"

Rósfrída flinched, fidgeting fiercely with the end of her braid. She was an honest child and hated to lie, so she valiantly looked off in another direction. "Ah, well, about that—"

"*Rósfrída.*"

"There's someone else on the mountain!" she blurted, words spilling out of her mouth like a creek in spring. "He's very nice and he has a stone so he can see me and-and-and we're in a *really* important discussion right now and I need to return to that; I'll talk with you later—" and with that, Rósfrída spun around and ducked away, retreating into a muted, blurred silhouette in the depths of the mirror. It was as close as she could come to running away, with their reflections bound as they were.

Svanhilda blinked. Once, twice, thrice.

"That's... new."

Björn lifted his head from the corner of the cave outside the vault, where he'd been nosing about in search of a snack. The cave had already been quite spacious, but Svanhilda's uncles had widened it even more, smoothing the floor and the walls. They had also provided several lamps that glowed without flame and could only be darkened by flinging a cloth over them. One corner of the cave was Björn's bed, where he slept if Rósfrída needed some space. It was well within view of the mirror, so if she felt alone, all she needed to do was glance out and see him there. The bed was made up of animal furs—mostly deer and elks—that Kiúli had either bought or hunted himself, and the far corner was where there were open crates of salted and smoked meats, provided by Ingiborg and her sisters, so Björn wouldn't be forced to hunt for himself all the time.

Each member of the family strove to show the depth of their gratitude to the bear who had saved and cared for Rósfrída.

"What's new?" Björn asked, after swallowing the mouthful of smoked herring he'd unearthed.

Svanhilda slowly made her way over to his pile of furs and sat down, staring absently at the mirror. "Rósfrída is apparently in the middle of a very important discussion with someone who can see her, so she can't talk to me right now."

There was a little silence.

"Huh. That *is* new." Björn grabbed another mouthful of herring, swallowed it back, and licked his snout thoughtfully. "Someone who can see her, you say?"

Svanhilda nodded. There was a restlessness in her heart and a burning behind her eyes. She wrapped her arms around herself and squeezed, trying to push the sensation back. It didn't feel like it was working very well.

"I'm not sure I like the implications of that."

"Nor I." Svanhilda rubbed the toe of her boot up and down the fur, staring intensely at it. "It would have to be something very powerful, wouldn't it? Or someone."

The bear nodded. After a thoughtful pause, he said, "How about we go and find out who this fellow is, and if we don't like him,

I bite his head off."

Svanhilda looked up, and saw Björn had meandered over to her and had sat down, lowering his head to be closer to her level. His eyes twinkled fondly at her, and she felt the burning behind her eyes drain away as a bright, happy warmth filled her heart. She flung herself at the bear again, throwing her arms around his neck and pressing her face against his thick fur.

She regretted this, as the fur was still wet, and thus smelled horribly. She reeled back and sneezed, a loud sound like that of a war-horn echoing off the mountains. This sneeze was followed by two others, each one louder than the one before. When she was done and was furiously wiping her watering eyes and nose, she peered over her arm at Björn.

He was making subdued snuffling sounds that the common bystander would mistake for something completely innocent. Unfortunately, Svanhilda had known Björn for the past seven years, and was quite aware that *particular* noise was his version of trying to disguise the fact he was laughing.

"Don't you *dare*," she grumbled. "This is all your fault."

The bear pointedly turned his head in another direction. "I have no idea what you're talking about."

"Of course, you don't," Svanhilda retorted primly, and the snuffling sounds resumed, his shoulder blades shaking.

This time, however, Svanhilda joined in, laughing quietly.

Somehow, she wasn't quite as worried for Rósfrída and whoever they would find at the other end of the reflection anymore.

Björn took the satchel of supplies through the mirror and came out with an expression that Svanhilda recognized as a frown.

"She wouldn't tell me anything either," he said, pinning the mirror with a hard look. "In fact, she took the satchel and hurried me back so swiftly I couldn't even get a good look at whoever she was talking to."

Svanhilda nodded solemnly, biting her lip again as she buried a hand in the thick fur of his shoulder. "Well, we'll just have to get a look at him the old-fashioned way, I suppose." She saw a hopeful look enter his eye, and she swatted the shoulder instead. "There will be no head-biting, unless it's absolutely necessary," she admonished firmly.

The bear's head drooped, though she firmly ignored it. She'd survived years of Rósfrída's pouty looks; a bear couldn't hold a candle to her sister.

They made their way back out into the world outside, and Björn put his nose to work, sniffing the air for a hint as to where their quarry lay. It was slow going, so they wandered through the forest for quite a while. At one point, Svanhilda did stumble across some mint, so she picked a fair share and put it in her pouch for Mother.

The sun was edging slowly towards the horizon, filling the woods with gold and shadow. They'd just come to a shallow little stream, hardly more than a rill, when Björn suddenly stopped in his tracks.

Svanhilda stopped immediately, her eyes seeking out Björn's, but he wouldn't look at her. He was frozen stiff, his blue eyes boring ahead. When Svanhilda followed his gaze, however, the trees blocked her view.

Beneath her hand buried in the fur of his shoulder, she could feel his muscles tense and tighten.

"Björn?" she began cautiously.

He didn't answer at first, yawning and clacking his teeth together once, twice.

A cold lump formed in the pit of Svanhilda's stomach, and she pressed her lips together tightly. Slowly, she straightened, and curled her fist in his pelt.

"*Ásbjörn.*" She put as much firmness and steadiness as she could manage into the name.

It worked. At least, it prompted him to speak.

"Stay back," he said, his voice guttural and thick, but there was an underlying emotion that she couldn't name at first.

"What's going on, Björn?" she whispered, but she obligingly took a step back, tucking herself a little behind his shoulder.

Björn relaxed slightly, but still his gaze never wavered.

"I don't know," he finally admitted, his voice still thick. "But there's someone up ahead, some one foreign and strong and *dangerous*."

It was then Svanhilda realized what lay beneath the tones of Björn's voice: *fear*.

The great white bear was terrified.

Svanhilda took a half step closer, pressing herself against the reassuringly solid warmth of Björn's ribs, and her free hand strayed towards the knife in her belt. "Is it an enemy?" she asked, voiced hushed.

The silence that followed this stretched out, and each second without an answer plucked at her nerves like clumsy fingers on the strings of a harp. Finally, however, Björn shook his head slightly, though his gaze stayed fixed straight ahead.

"No." He said it slowly, thoughtfully, trying to pull together what he was feeling into words. "It's strong, and angry. It's not cruel. Not… malicious. Not like… others."

Others?

Svanhilda drew in a shaky breath. "Is Rósfrída in danger?"

Björn shook his head again. "I can't imagine so. If it weren't for the anger, I'd almost say it was… wholesome, perhaps?"

The breath came out again, equally shaky, but just a smidgeon less terrified. "Very well. What… what should we do, then?"

"Wait," the bear replied. "Until this storm—whatever it is— has passed, there's very little else we can do."

CHAPTER 3

S o? What do you have to say for yourself?" the man demanded sharply, shifting his stance enough so light illuminated half of his face, highlighting a scornfully arched eyebrow. "What did you do that you've stolen Funi's scent?"

Tryggvi sat silently, hardly daring to breathe. He had no idea what was going on, and he'd lived long enough to learn that if you don't understand the situation, it's sometimes better to keep your mouth shut, than open it and risk making things worse.

The strange man began to look Tryggvi up and down, the eyebrow arching higher. "Though, I must admit, while you're not exactly a helpless kitten, you don't look like you'd be much of a threat to someone like Fu—" The word stopped abruptly, and keen golden eyes narrowed on the amber stone hanging around Tryggvi's neck.

"Ahhhhhhhh." The sound left the man in a long sigh, turning to a faint chuckle at the end, and his posture suddenly relaxed. The heavy air of *threat* suddenly vanished, and Tryggvi felt like he could properly draw breath for the first time since the man stepped out from behind the tree. "Well, *that* explains it, I suppose."

Tryggvi blinked and glanced down at Allvaldi. The cat had settled somewhat in his lap, his fur no longer puffed out defensively, but his green eyes never strayed from their visitor. Reassured that Allvaldi was no longer quite so frightened, Tryggvi glanced up to see he was once again the subject of appraisal from the other man.

With a quick breath and marshalling of his nerve, Tryggvi raised his chin and declared boldly, "I'm sorry, sir, but I'm afraid I have no idea what you are talking about, or even who you are."

"Ah, yes, quite. Rather remiss of me," the man remarked, amusement in his tone. He bowed towards Tryggvi, fire-orange hair sweeping over his shoulder.

"First, I was passing through on my way to visit a friend. I'm terribly sorry for accusing you unjustly, but it's not particularly pleasant to turn the corner and expect to see an old friend and find something *quite* different. I'm afraid I acted a bit hastily in my shock."

"Ah." Tryggvi swallowed hard and bowed his head back. "I'd imagine so. And who *are* you?"

"Me?" The man flashed a grin and bowed again. "You may call me Refskegg."

Tryggvi blinked, and the words left his mouth before he could reign them in. "But… you don't *have* a beard."

It was true. While the man had hair aplenty on his head, none of it was on his chin.

Refskegg snorted and moved his head in a way that indicated he was dramatically rolling his eyes. "Of course not! Can't stand the things, terribly itchy. 'Twas Funi's idea of a joke."

"I see." This was not entirely the truth, as Tryggvi did *not* entirely see, but he did understand friends with an odd sense of humor—Allvaldi, for example. "The same Funi you were looking for?"

"The very same! He's an old friend of mine." Refskegg tilted his head to one side thoughtfully. "You might have heard of him—Austvindr, he's sometimes called."

"Austvind—" Tryggvi nearly choked. "You mean, the East Wind?"

"The very same."

"With all due respect," Tryggvi said slowly, "what, by all the tides, made you think I was *the East Wind himself?*"

"True, I was rather curious myself as to why you smelled like him, and I didn't like the implications." Refskegg took several steps forward and bent over, pointing straight at the little amber pendant hanging from Tryggvi's neck. Instinctively, Tryggvi's hold tightened on it protectively, and Refskegg's brows lifted in amusement as his mouth curled into a faint smirk.

"But that," he continued calmly, despite the smirk that still sat smugly on his face, "explains the whole thing *quite* handily, though

I'm rather curious as to how it found its way into your hands."

Tryggvi stroked his forefinger over the surface, the long familiar patterns of smoothness and grooves helping to settle him somewhat. "It was a gift from my mother," he reported honestly. "She said it came on a merchant ship from a faraway land. She had elven-blood, and she told me that she sensed it had a great and good power."

Refskegg hummed thoughtfully, his eyebrow arching again. When he spoke, it was quiet, almost as if he were speaking to himself. "Ah, so that's where it went. Good to know! I'll have to tell him. He'll be pleased, I think. And she'll be more at ease, for sure."

Tryggvi raised his eyebrows and lifted his stone a little higher. "You know the owner of this stone—and it's the *East Wind?*"

"Mm, you could say that," the man said, "though it's been quite a long time since he, ah, lost it, shall we say?"

Tryggvi took a deep breath, but he knew what he should do, so he quickly nudged Allvaldi off his lap. Allvaldi greatly disapproved of this but didn't quite dare to make too much of a ruckus in such powerful company. Instead, he restrained himself to bestowing his nastiest glare upon Tryggvi.

Tryggvi didn't notice, or maybe he was immune to such glares by now. Instead, he quickly rose to his feet and bowed his head, slipping the thong over his head and holding the pendant towards the man. "Then, it should be returned to whom it belongs. Here, take it, and give it to him, with my apologies."

The man laughed and reached out only to push the stone back into Tryggvi's grasp. "How can I return it to whom it belongs when he is holding it even now?"

Tryggvi's head shot up, his eyes wide. "—But—"

Refskegg shook his head, a grin sharp as knives darting across his face. "He wouldn't take it back; in fact, he'd be rather insulted if I tried to give it to him. Besides the fact that it, well, it'd just be *odd.* Not quite sure how that would work." For a moment, he almost seemed to shudder, but came back to himself with a quick shake of his head. "No, he lost it fair and square and willingly, and cast it upon the world to find a master worth serving. It seems it has found one indeed."

"Now," Refskegg said, rising and stepping back, "I fear I have to be going, as it seems Funi is *not* here—and I really *do* have to find him. My wife will *not* be pleased if I tarry overlong, considering I put her in charge in my absence. Therefore, fare—"

"Wait!" Rósfrída called out from the dagger. "Did you say you were friends with the East Wind?"

Tryggvi started violently, almost dropping the dagger. Rósfrída, being in possession of rather limited vision and very confused as to what was going on, had decided waiting and listening was the best course of action. For Tryggvi's part, he'd been so focused on trying to deal with the situation and get out of it with his body intact, he had completely forgotten why he was holding his knife in the first place.

On Refskegg's part, both his eyebrows shot up nearly to his hairline, mouth open in confusion. "I'm sorry," he finally managed, "but did that knife of yours just *talk*?"

"Nope!" Rósfrída chirped. "I'm trapped in a mirror and need a mirrored surface to see anything Outside."

"Well," Refskegg said gently, more gently than his tone had been since he first spoke, "you've met with a terrible fate, haven't you."

"It's not so bad," Rósfrída said, though to ears as keen as Refskegg's, the slight quaver in her voice was quite plain. "I can talk to my sister, and Tryggvi can see me with that special stone of his, so, please tell Master Austvindr that I'm very, very grateful for his gift!"

The man's face softened, and he smiled—a warm, kind, benevolent thing—and bowed his head. "I'll be sure to pass on your gratitude, little one." He lifted his head once more and grinned brightly. "I'm sure he'll be very pleased it was of great help to you."

Rósfrída smiled back at him, bouncing a little happily. "I have Björn, too; he's a bear, except he's not, he was a boy first—" She gasped. "That's right! I wanted to ask you—you said you know the East Wind?"

Refskegg nodded. "Indeed, I do. We're old friends."

"Then," Rósfrída twisted the end of her braid furiously, "do you know anything about how the curse was broken on Prince Býulfr? Because my friend has been cursed to be a white bear, and we can't figure out how to help him."

The man rubbed his chin thoughtfully, silent for a long moment. "I'm afraid…" he said at last, slowly and thoughtfully, "I can't be of much assistance. I wasn't *personally* involved in that affair, and I don't remember too much of what Funi told me. I'd ask Funi for you, but the man has always had a bit of wanderlust, and it might take me a while yet to track him down…"

"Oh." Rósfrída said quietly, and bit her lip, blinking furiously to combat the pricklings of disappointment that laid siege to her eyes. "I see…"

"However!" Refskegg forestalled loudly, sticking one finger in the air, "there *is* someone I know who *was* involved in that particular adventure, and I believe…" he turned slowly in a circle, drawing in a deep breath as he did so, before sighing in satisfaction, "he happens to be nearby. On this very mountain, in fact."

He paused, mouth twisting and eyebrows lifting. "Convenient, that." He tapped his raised finger against his chin, eyes narrowed in thought. "I'd bet Funi's foot the Old Man had something to do with it. He's better than *me* at sticking his nose into suspicious business, and that's saying something."

He rummaged around in the purse hanging from his belt, finally retrieving something with a faint, "*A-ha!*" He lifted the item to his lips and blew faintly, whispering something so quietly not even Allvaldi could quite make it out—not that he'd admit it. Then, Refskegg held it out to Tryggvi.

Tryggvi looked at it and raised an eyebrow. It was a leaf.

"Take this token and give it to the elf-bard named Flosi, with my compliments. He should be able to help you."

With a shrug, Tryggvi took it, putting it away carefully in his own purse. He'd never really thought of a single leaf as particularly important, but if it could help him get Ásbjörn back, he'd treat it as if it were made from spun glass.

"I had best be off," Refskegg said once the leaf was tucked away. "But best of luck with breaking the curse on your friend—and on you, little one." His eyes bored sharply into Tryggvi as he said this.

Tryggvi didn't even flinch. He lifted his chin and stared right back, forcing all his determination to help Rósfrída into his gaze, hoping that this strange man would glean some of it.

After a long moment, a satisfied smile settled on Refskegg's face, as if he were pleased with what he had seen. He tipped his head in a nod, then turned his gaze to the mountain, his expression turning thoughtful. "One last word before I go."

His tone was different, this time—serious and full of warning, yet almost detached—as if, at that moment, he was not quite *there*.

"There is a foul scent on this mountain, one I do not like. A scent of betrayal, and blood; the mountain itself cries out for justice." A sharp frown was on his face, and a golden fire burned in the depths of his eyes. "It's been a long time since I smelled such a scent as this…"

He sighed, eyes narrowing, mouth twisting further. "… a long time."

He came back to himself with a shake of his head, turning back to face his audience.

Tryggvi, Allvaldi, and Rósfrída all stared at him, very confused.

He arched an eyebrow back at them, as if to say "what?", before speaking. "Needless to say, you needs must be *very* careful. It seems like there is a tangled net here—secrets dark and deep buried in the heart of this mountain. Still, that stone of yours shall serve you well, and with my apprentice's help, I believe you shall be fine—so long as you keep your wits about you."

He half-turned to leave, paused, then grinned—sharp and sly as a fox. "I'll be going now," he said, then turned fully back to Tryggvi and lifted his arm, pointing off to the right. "But once I am gone, walk straight in that direction. You might just find something interesting waiting for you."

With that, Refskegg bowed once and strode away, his red, fur-lined cloak billowing behind him. Before any of the three watching could blink, he'd rounded a tree and was gone.

There was a long silence.

What, by all my glorious whiskers, was that? Allvaldi finally managed. He was not often at a loss for words, so Refskegg, Tryggvi mused, was even more impressive than he had originally thought.

"I…" Tryggvi thought for a minute. "…Honestly? I have no idea."

"He seemed rather nice," Rósfrída said thoughtfully. "Once he stopped threatening to slice you to ribbons, Tryggvi. After all, he gave us quite a bit of help!"

Tryggvi snorted, grinning. "So, what you're saying is, once he stopped being heart-stoppingly frightening, he ended up being a decent fellow."

"Pretty much, I suppose," Rósfríða replied, and burst into giggles. Tryggvi followed her a second later, laughing so hard he ended up having to lean back against the tree before he fell over.

Allvaldi eyed the pair scornfully, having little use for hysterical two-legged beings, and set about a task of much greater import: namely, smoothing down any fur left ruffled by his momentary discomfiture.

When the laughter had finally died down into incoherent wheezes that had eventually trickled off into satisfied sighs, Tryggvi tipped his head back against the tree and smiled thoughtfully.

"You're right, though… he did end up helping us a lot, even if he was utterly terrifying at the beginning. What are the chances?"

"Maybe…" Rósfríða said tentatively, "…maybe, the Lea of Flame has been guiding us."

Tryggvi smiled down at his reflection, where sea-green eyes shone hopefully back at him, and felt his own hope burn brighter in his chest. "You know, my lady… you just might be right."

'All this is very touching,' Allvaldi piped up, having long since finished his primping, 'but didn't that Refskegg character mention something about finding something interesting off to the right?'

"So he did, my good fellow, so he did," Tryggvi grinned, pushing off the tree and stretching the kinks out of his muscles. "Shall we go see what it is?"

Björn took one long deep sniff, following it up with a couple short, quick snuffles to be certain. "The presence—whatever *that* was—seems to be fading. The coast is probably clear."

"Shall we go check out the source of that unnerving laughter, then?" Svanhilda asked thoughtfully, eyeing the distance between the

121

sun and the horizon. "I'm not keen on facing whatever *that* was in the dark, but it'll be another couple hours before the sun sets."

Björn shook his head and rolled his shoulders. "Let's do it, then."

However, they'd taken all of two steps before someone stepped out from amongst the trees, and they froze in their tracks.

It was a tall young man with flaxen hair in two thick braids and a chin yet un-bearded from youth, handsome and cheerful and loose-limbed. At his feet trotted a forest cat with its tail held high—a truly magnificent specimen with a long gold coat and bright leaf-green eyes.

Svanhilda stopped and stared at him because he was smiling down at the blade of his dagger and chatting as he walked.

Björn stopped for an entirely different reason.

The cat spotted them first, as the young man was rather enamored with the blade of his dagger. He glanced up at the man and meowed loudly, and the man immediately looked up from his knife.

A boy and a bear stared at each other across the surface of a small stream.

Slowly, the young man sheathed his dagger, and took one step forward.

Björn didn't move.

Tryggvi took one more step.

The bear remained still, as if he'd been turned into a statue carved from the mountain itself.

And then—Tryggvi leapt straight across the rill and barreled into his brother, arms winding around his neck and face burying itself in thick white fur.

Björn still hadn't moved, feeling as if all breath and movement and thought had been driven from his body. Perhaps it had.

"I found you," Tryggvi breathed against Björn's fur, in the strained sort of voice that comes just before a sob. "I found you."

After a long moment of stillness, Björn heaved a great sigh, and let his head droop. "So you did. But you should have stayed away."

Tryggvi didn't move. "*Why?*"

Björn shut his eyes, shuddering as he finally forced the words out that had been haunting his mind for a decade. "Can you not see what

I've become? I cannot be the brother you deserve, not like this."

Everything was quiet.

Then Tryggvi laughed. It was strained, and choking, and half-full of sobs, but it was still a laugh. "Who says? *I* say you *are*, and that's all that matters."

Slowly, Tryggvi unwound his arms from around Björn's neck and stepped back so he could look him in the eye. He bowed his head and reached out, tentatively laying his hands against the bear's jaw. "…You'll *always* be my brother, Ásbjörn… as long as you still want me."

For a moment, Björn didn't move. Then, slowly, he lifted his head and opened his eyes, and pressed his forehead against Tryggvi's bowed one.

"Silly little Tryggvi," he rumbled quietly. "Have you forgotten? There is nothing in all the world that could make me not want you for my brother."

CHAPTER 4

S o, you met a strange man in the woods, and he gave you a leaf
and told you to give it to an elf," Björn repeated.

Tryggvi nodded firmly.

'*See, your brother agrees with me,*' Allvaldi pointed out. '*It sounds insane.*'

"Be that as it may, Allvaldi," Tryggvi said, glancing down at the cat sitting on his foot, "it's the only lead we have."

"That is very true," Svanhilda agreed, though her frown betrayed her uncertainty. "And what's the name of the elf?"

"Flosi the Bard!" Rósfrída piped in from the surface of the rill. Tryggvi repeated this for the benefit of his brother.

As soon as the bear heard it, he raised his head in interest. "An elven bard? And this…"

"Refskegg," Tryggvi supplied.

Björn nodded his thanks. "Refskegg said he's on this mountain?"

Tryggvi nodded. "That's right."

"Well…" Björn glanced over at Svanhilda. "I've run into an elf carrying a harp and singing around the forests several times over the years."

"I've never seen him, but I *have* heard him singing several times," she concurred, then glanced down at the surface of the water. "What about you, Rósfrída?"

Her sister hummed, bouncing up and down a little as she thought. "I think I've heard a song once or twice, and caught a glimpse of someone in the reflections, but he's avoided my gaze rather well."

Svanhilda frowned at this, but Rósfrída grinned. "However," she said, "I have an idea. Why don't we just ask Eylir?"

It was several seconds before anyone replied. Svanhilda was in the stunned stupor of one who has realized they'd missed an obvious answer, while Tryggvi and Allvaldi were silent out of confusion. Björn was quiet because he couldn't hear Rósfrída, which was making communication a little more difficult than anticipated.

"That…" Svanhilda finally said, "is a very good idea. If there's another elf on the mountain, Eylir's sure to know them!"

"Who?" Björn asked.

Svanhilda ignored him for the moment, and leaned over the surface of the water, blowing a kiss at her sister's reflection. "Thank you, Rósfrída! What would I do without you?"

"Be dreadfully bored and hopelessly lost," Rósfrída replied, smug as Allvaldi, which was quite the feat.

Svanhilda merely smiled, a warm and tender thing. "Quite right, and a lot of other equally miserable things besides. I'll get out my mirror once we get to Eylir's grove?"

"I'll be waiting!" Rósfrída promised, and Svanhilda stepped away, purpose and hope riding high on her shoulders.

"Follow me!" she called and began running off through the woods. Tryggvi and Björn glanced at each other, bewildered, but took off after her, one sprinting, the other in a shambling run.

"Where are we going?" Björn called.

Svanhilda smiled over her shoulder. "To see an old friend!"

"You didn't say your friend lived half the mountain away," Tryggvi panted, leaning against a tree.

"It's not that far," Svanhilda laughed, though she too was a bit out of breath. "Only about half an hour's walk. We still have another hour of daylight."

"Still, it's far enough away that it's out of my usual prowling grounds," Björn noted, looking up briefly from where he was lapping thirstily at a stream. "It's probably why I've never met this Eylir fellow before."

"He's also somewhat shy," Svanhilda added, digging around in her purse. "And it's not like he's here all the time." She found the mirror and pulled it out, smiling into it.

"We're here, Rósfrída."

Rósfrída blinked to attention and smiled excitedly. "Oh, wonderful! It's been a bit since I've seen Eylir."

"I think he was back home for a while," Svanhilda said. "But I was nearby not too long ago and saw him from a distance, so he should be here."

"What if he isn't?" Tryggvi asked curiously.

Svanhilda bit her lip. There was a long silence.

"We'll figure that out when we come to it," she said at last, and turned to go into the grove.

Björn and Tryggvi gave each other a long look behind her back, then Tryggvi grinned, shrugged, and hurried after Svanhilda. Björn simply shook his head, huffed once in amusement, and shambled after them.

Svanhilda took three steps into the grove, cupped her hands around her mouth, and called out, "Eylir! Eylir, it's me, Svanhilda! We need to talk to you!"

Everything was quiet, the silence only broken by the sound of the wind rustling the branches of the trees.

Then, from amongst the shadows of the grove, out stepped a little elf-child clad in white and green, and he ran forward and flung his arms happily around Svanhilda's waist. She smiled down at him and crouched down, hugging him fondly in return.

"It's been a while since you've visited, Svanhilda!" he said happily.

She laughed and patted his head fondly. "And despite all that, you haven't grown at all."

Eylir pulled back and gave her a serious look. "I've grown a little bit since we met!"

Svanhilda leaned down and booped him playfully on the nose. "Have you really? Are you certain?"

Eylir ducked away from her hand, but he was giggling quietly. Svanhilda smiled fondly down at him and tapped the surface of her handheld mirror. "Rósfrída says hello as well."

The boy smiled sweetly and raised a hand in a little wave. Rósfrída waved enthusiastically back, even though he couldn't see her.

Then the boy looked up at Svanhilda, tilting his head curiously. "What do you need me for? Did you get in trouble again? Do you need my help?"

"Something like that," Svanhilda said with a wry smile, before gesturing over at Tryggvi. "My friend here was told to talk to an elf named Flosi the Bard who dwells on this mountain. Is that so?"

Eylir turned to examine Tryggvi, green eyes solemnly looking the man up and down. As soon as Flosi's name left Svanhilda's lips, however, his entire expression changed, his face lighting up like the sun.

"Yes, it is! My brother Flosi does live here—for now, anyway. He says he's doing a favor for a friend. Do you want me to fetch him for you?"

The three adults who were not mirror-bound exchanged an excited look, and Svanhilda turned back to Eylir. "We'd like that very much, thank you."

Eylir smiled happily and walked over to the nearest tree, pressing one hand against the trunk, and closing his eyes, whispering quietly underneath his breath. After a long moment, he trotted back, chin lifted in satisfaction.

"Brother Flosi says he's coming, and he'll be here soon," he reported solemnly, then crouched down, sticking a small hand out toward Allvaldi.

Allvaldi sniffed it, and deeming it acceptable, permitted the boy to pet his ears.

"I didn't know you had a brother who lived nearby," Svanhilda said. "Is his grove here on the mountain?"

"Oh, no," Eylir shook his head, though his focus remained bent upon the all-important business of scratching beneath Allvaldi's chin. "Brother Flosi doesn't have a grove!"

Tryggvi raised his eyebrows in surprise. He himself had not enough elven blood to have been given a grove of his own, but he'd soaked in all the knowledge of his mother's ancestors that he could. He'd never heard of an elf who had been born without a grove. "Truly? Did he use to have one, and just lost it?"

Eylir shook his head again. "No. Mother said he was born into the winds, and therefore he goes wherever the wind blows, taking care of all the forests he comes across."

Tryggvi blinked. "Huh."

Before he could ask anything else, another man stepped out of the grove. He was tall—over a head taller than Tryggvi himself, who was not precisely the shortest of specimens—and lean of frame. His hair was bright gold, with long braids that were bound together in a great knot at his shoulder blades, and his green eyes were sharp and keen.

As soon as he stepped out of the shadow of the trees and into the light, Eylir had bounced up and trotted over to him, hugging his much older brother's leg. Flosi, or so Tryggvi assumed, smiled down at his little brother, settling a hand on feathery flaxen hair.

"Hello there, baby brother," he said fondly. "What do you need me for?" As he spoke, he glanced up and eyed the three other adults. He glanced at the mirror as he did so, and for a moment, Tryggvi could have sworn that a flash of sorrow and guilt crossed the elf's face. It was gone the next second, smoothed over like a hand passing over fur or fabric, so there was no way for Tryggvi to be certain.

Eylir stepped back a little, and reached up for his brother's hand instead, tugging it gently and pointing at Tryggvi. "That man there— the one with elf blood—he said he was told to talk to you."

Flosi's eyebrows rose at that, and he glanced at Tryggvi with renewed interest. "Well now!" he said. "You seem to be an interesting fellow—and a good one at that, if you have such a fine specimen of a companion." He nodded down at Allvaldi with a smile. "You can trust an elf-cat to be an excellent judge of character."

Allvaldi stared back at Flosi for a long second, before turning back to Tryggvi with an air of great importance and solemnity.

'I like this elf. He seems to be greatly intelligent. I say we trust him.'

"Well, with such a stunning recommendation as that, how can we not?" Tryggvi laughed, before facing the bard and digging in his purse for the leaf he had been given.

"We met someone, a man named Refskegg."

At this, Flosi's brows rose in surprise, though he refrained from saying anything.

"He told us to give you this, with his compliments." Tryggvi held out the leaf.

Flosi plucked it from his fingers, lifting it up and examining it closely. "It was Master Refskegg, sure enough," he finally said at length. "What in the world was he doing here?"

"He was searching for the Austvindr," Tryggvi reported.

Flosi nodded. "That makes sense." He glanced over the leaf again, then tucked it in his own purse, folding his arms expectantly.

"Very well—why do you need my aid so badly?"

Svanhilda and Tryggvi looked at each other, and after a moment Svanhilda spoke. "This bear, here, is under a curse, and we don't know how to help him."

"Refskegg said you were involved in the breaking of the curse on Prince Býulfr," Tryggvi added, "and we were wondering if you would be able to figure out how to break this one."

Flosi stared hard at the bear, then finally sighed and shook his head. "The curse on that man is of dwarf-make, while the one on Býulfr was quite another matter entirely. I know a little about dwarves and their skills, but not enough to combat something like this."

Tryggvi felt a stone beginning to settle in his gut, but before despair could stick more than a toe inside his heart, Flosi strode forward and crouched in front of Björn. He stared at the torque for a long moment, before reaching out and tapping the torque sharply with one finger.

"There are threads of power on this torque, threads tied directly to the one who cast the curse. You'd have to sever that connection, but if you could manage it—well, I'd imagine you'd be able to remove it easily. This torque was not made to be a curse."

"So?" Björn asked eagerly. "How do you break such a connection?"

Flosi met his gaze solemnly for a long moment. "… I have no idea."

Björn's head drooped, Tryggvi and Rósfrída groaned, and Svanhilda bit her lip.

Tryggvi clenched his fists, trying to resist the urge to pace, nervous energy building in his limbs. They'd come so far, and there was so little he could do to help. "Is there a way we can find out how?"

"I wouldn't know," Flosi said thoughtfully, slowly rising back to his feet, still eyeing the torque. "The powers of the dwarves are a deeply ingrained part of their selves, and the dwarves are a secretive folk. I have wandered all over these lands, and known many dwarves, and I've never heard even the faintest whispers regarding such a thing. My guess would be only their most revered elders would have such knowledge in their keeping, and they would not part with it easily."

"So, even if we asked our mother," Svanhilda said, slowly, "she wouldn't be able to tell us?"

"You can always ask, but I doubt she would have an answer for you," Flosi said solemnly.

No one spoke for a long while. Svanhilda had wrapped her arms about herself, biting her lip and looking away. Björn's head was hanging, and his eyes were closed, as if to shut out the world. Tryggvi stared at the ground, gaining little comfort from the way Allvaldi rubbed against his legs.

Rósfrída watched from the mirror, face pale and hands clasped against her heart. It made Tryggvi's heart hurt even more—if he felt helpless, standing here in the free air, how must she feel, locked in her room, only able to see whatever was caught in a reflection?

"So?" Tryggvi asked, forcing the words past the great stone in his throat. "Is that it, then? Is there no one who could give us an answer?"

Flosi bent down and slowly stroked his hand down Allvaldi's back, frowning heavily in thought. "It would have to be someone with a vast store of knowledge and power. While such individuals certainly exist, they are not easy to track down. It could potentially take months before I could manage to track down Finnvard, for instance—or I could stumble across him tomorrow."

Tryggvi swallowed hard. Months? Surely, if it ended with Björn's freedom, such a wait was worth it, but—"Is there truly no other way?"

Flosi merely frowned down at the ground, continuing to stroke Allvaldi's fur. Then, a small hand reached out, and Eylir tentatively tugged at his brother's sleeve.

"Father is very old and powerful," he said quietly, "and he knows a great many things."

"That…" Flosi said slowly, something like hope beginning to brighten his eyes, "is very, very true."

A bright grin stretched across his face, and he swept Eylir up into his arms and spun him around, laughing merrily. Eylir giggled along and was still giggling when Flosi swung him onto his hip and grinned over at the others.

"Go home tonight; it's getting dark," he said, "and there are things that lurk in the dark on this mountain—nasty, unpleasant things." He eyed Björn knowingly, but Björn turned his head away, refusing to meet the keen gaze of the elf. So Flosi looked at the others instead, confidence and hope draped over his shoulders like a mantle. "Go home, my lady Svanhilda, and ask your mother what she knows; but if she cannot answer, do not despair! Simply gather here tomorrow when the morning is young, and you may yet get your answer!"

And with that announcement, before any of the others could move or even respond, the bard turned on his heel and strode off into the woods, taking his brother with him. Within moments, both had vanished into the evening shadows that lay thick beneath the trees.

Everyone stared after them. Finally, Rósfrída spoke, her eyes shining hopefully. "Well, that's certainly more than nothing, right?"

"Yes," Svanhilda said, smiling down at Björn, whose head was held higher than she had seen in a long time. "It is a great deal more than nothing, I'd say."

Tryggvi rubbed the heel of his palm into one of his eyes, wiping away the tear that had gathered onto his lashes. It was too soon to cry—they'd made progress, yes, but Björn was still a bear, and there was no guarantee that this lead would bear fruit.

Still, it was, as Rósfrída and Svanhilda had said, more than nothing at all, and it filled his heart with more hope than he'd had in years.

'*See?*' Allvaldi said smugly, with a flick of his tail. '*I said I liked that elf.*'

Tryggvi laughed and crouched down to rub at Allvaldi's ears. "So you did, my friend. So you did."

"I'm glad you could help them," Eylir announced, wrapping his arms around his brother's neck for security as they walked. "Rósfrída and Svanhilda are my friends, but they need watching," he said solemnly, with a sage nod of his head. "They tend to get in a lot of trouble."

"Is that so, Eylir?" Flosi laughed. "Well, I am certainly glad to help their friend. And, if we can figure out a way to help the man beneath the bear, then we might be able to help your friend Rósfrída as well."

Eylir perked up at this. "Really? She's been stuck in there for an awfully long time. I can't see her, but I think it must make her sad."

"Really," Flosi promised him. "With any luck, you should be able to see her soon."

"That would be nice," Eylir said, and then yawned sleepily, nestling his head down on his brother's shoulder. He dropped off quickly, leaving Flosi alone with his thoughts.

He'd been on this mountain for ten years, now. Not a particularly great expanse in the life of an elf, hardly worth notice to most of his kind; but when one is forced to stand by and watch someone trapped and in misery, even the shortest period of time could feel like an eternity.

Until now, Björn had not wanted help, believing there was no hope for any escape from his prison. And Flosi knew quite well that unless someone wished to be helped, the efforts of anyone else would never bear fruit.

Still, it didn't make it any less painful to stand by and watch and do nothing.

"If this works," he whispered into the eventide, "and Björn is freed, then all my years of waiting and hoping will not be in vain. And if through my help Rósfrída is freed… then perhaps I may begin to atone for my failure to protect her, at last."

It might be too much to hope for, but Flosi had always been the sort to strive unvaryingly for the unattainable.

As long as there was a way, then he'd find it—for the boy and girl who'd been bound for so long, so they might once more breathe the air in freedom.

Chapter 5

e should stay with you at your house," Björn said firmly. "It's far more comfortable there."

"He should be spending his time with you," Svanhilda countered, just as resolutely. "He's spent a long time waiting to come to this mountain, and it wasn't to visit me."

"I live in a cave."

"You're his brother!"

"How long has this been going on now?" Rósfrída asked Tryggvi, watching the commotion from his dagger with wide, fascinated eyes.

"Probably close to a quarter-hour, now," Tryggvi said thoughtfully, "with no sign of stopping anytime soon."

"They're both too nice by half." Rósfrída shook her head sagely. "One will wear down the other eventually, but it'll probably be dark by then."

"They've done this before?"

Rósfrída smiled despite her sigh of exasperation. "Several times."

"And they're just going to continue until one manages to convince the other?"

Rósfrída nodded, and Tryggvi clicked his tongue. "Well, we can't wait until then. You heard what the bard said; I don't want to meet whatever it is that lurks in the dark on this mountain." With that, he straightened his shoulders, lifted his chin, and marched forward.

"Tryggvi is my little brother, and it's my responsibility to see that he's comfortable—"

"Tryggvi," the man in question cut in loudly, "is a man in his own right, and can make his own decisions."

Silence fell. Svanhilda coughed, Björn huffed, and both looked away sheepishly.

Rósfríða giggled from the safety of her dagger. "They can be rather silly, can't they?" she whispered, just loud enough that only Tryggvi would catch her words.

"So they can," he whispered back. "If you will give me a second?"

"Of course."

Tryggvi slipped his dagger back inside its sheath and clapped his hands once. "All right. Since I don't want to impose upon your hospitality, Svanhilda, I'll be staying with my brother in his cave."

Svanhilda sent Björn a triumphant look. The bear opened his mouth, but a quick kick to the leg made Björn reconsider.

"Great, that's settled!" Tryggvi said. "Now, shall we escort Svanhilda home?"

The walk was quiet, everyone's mind far too distracted for conversation. Allvaldi was the only one oblivious to the tension, and was in fact quite content, since Björn had agreed to let the cat ride upon his back. He spent the entire walk curled up on the bear's shoulder blades, catching up on a long-overdue nap.

The sun was hovering above the edge of the horizon when they arrived, and Svanhilda moved to go inside. Just as she touched the handle, however, she paused, and glanced back over her shoulder.

"Shall we meet tomorrow in front of Eylir's grove?"

Björn and Tryggvi shared a glance. "I suppose that would be wisest," the bear ventured after a few moments' thought. "Until tomorrow morning, then."

'Excellent,' Allvaldi said, hopping off the bear's back and stretching. He flicked his tail once, twice, licked a paw, and marched towards the house.

"Allvaldi?" Tryggvi asked. "Just where do you think you're going?"

The cat shot Tryggvi a look over his shoulder. *'I would have thought it was obvious. The lady has very generously offered her hospitality, and I am not so foolish as to let such an opportunity pass me by.'*

Tryggvi rolled his eyes. "Svanhilda, do you mind looking after my cat for tonight?"

Allvaldi sniffed at the implication that he would need any sort of "looking after", but Svanhilda merely smiled and nodded her assent.

"Then, Allvaldi," Tryggvi bowed, his tone dripping with a mockery of deferent solemnity, "you have my permission to stay."

The look Allvaldi shot him was nearly enough to wither a man on the spot; luckily, Tryggvi was made of sterner stuff. By this time, Svanhilda had gone inside, but courteously held the door open. The cat proceeded to saunter through the opening with all the grace and pomp of a king, pausing at the threshold to give Tryggvi one last look over his shoulder.

'Enjoy your cave.'

And with a flick of his tail, he darted inside.

>>*<< · >>*<< · >>*<<

"Is that a cat, darling?" Ingiborg said, looking up from where she sat spinning by the fire.

"Yes." Svanhilda sat down on the straw by her mother's feet, leaning against the legs of Ingiborg's carved wooden chair. "Björn's brother came up to visit, and his cat decided he'd stay here for the night."

"And I assume Björn's brother is a man and not a bear?" Ingiborg said calmly, not looking up from her work.

Svanhilda hummed in affirmation. "…You don't seem very surprised."

At this, Ingiborg glanced over at her daughter, an amused smile on her face. "I grew up amongst the forges of the dwarves, darling. I know the difference between a talking beast and a man. Besides," she laughed, "I have thirteen brothers and sisters; it takes a great deal to surprise me."

Svanhilda giggled, and Ingiborg patted her on the head before returning her focus to her spindle. Allvaldi, having completed a swift inspection of his new environs, made his way over to Svanhilda and claimed her lap as his own, occasionally reaching out to bat a Ingiborg's bobbing spindle.

Svanhilda ran her fingers through his fur, letting her mind drift as she stared into the flames of the hearth. Finally, she got up the nerve to speak.

"Mother… have you ever heard of a way to sever a dwarf's connection to his power?"

Ingiborg glanced up again, startled. "No, I've never heard of such a thing. Why do you ask?"

Svanhilda hummed again, biting her lip nervously. It was as Flosi had guessed—Mother had no answers—so their main hope lay in whether Flosi and Eylir's father could provide some insight.

"We're going to try and break Björn's curse: Rósfrída, his brother, and I," she admitted quietly, not looking away from the fire's incandescent dance.

There was silence for several moments as Ingiborg pondered this. "I see," she said at length. "I wish you all good fortune and success."

That, finally, was enough to drag Svanhilda's gaze away from the fire, and she glanced up at her mother in shock. "Is that all you're going to say?"

Ingiborg raised a delicate eyebrow. "Do you wish for me to say more?" she asked, amused. "Very well. Remember that, when you succeed, Björn will have to wait until your father returns to obtain our consent."

Svanhilda's eyes went very, very wide, and she snapped her gaze back to the fire, trying to convince herself it was the source of the heat crawling in her cheeks. "I have no idea what you are referring to, mother."

Ingiborg laughed softly. "Lying does not become us, darling."

Svanhilda did not bother to deign that with an answer.

>>*<< · >>*<< · >>*<<

Björn, Tryggvi thought in the warm, sleepy daze of early morning, *makes a very excellent pillow.*

He rolled over slightly to avoid the light filtering through the waterfall-curtain at the entrance to the cave, curling closer to his brother and burying his face in Björn's thick, warm fur.

Then something wet and dreadfully cold touched the back of his neck, and Tryggvi shot awake with a yelp.

"I take it back," Tryggvi muttered, rubbing away the dampness

137

Björn's nose had left on his skin as he glared resentfully at his brother. "You make a terrible pillow, indeed."

Björn, if his huffs of amusement were anything to go by, did not seem terribly offended by this. Instead, he merely nudged Tryggvi with his side.

"It's morning, and we have to be going," he rumbled.

Tryggvi rubbed a hand over his face and nodded, yawning loudly. "Right," he finally replied. "Let's get going, then."

He stood up and stretched, and once he'd stepped away from where Björn lay, the bear rose to his feet with a great shake of his shoulders and a massive yawn that put Tryggvi's to shame.

"I'm going to catch myself some breakfast in the pool outside," Björn informed his brother. "I'd suggest you get something for yourself and meet me outside."

Tryggvi was yawning again, so he merely responded with a nod, and Björn shuffled his way over to the waterfall and dove through the spray. That left Tryggvi alone in the cave.

After a quick rummage through his satchel, he'd come up with some flat bread, dried venison, and cheese, and set about consuming his breakfast. His stomach felt like an empty hole, so he finished quickly, and stood up, wiping his greasy hands on his trousers.

It was then he noticed a flash of red in the mirror on the far wall, and he grinned, quickly striding over toward it.

Rósfrída didn't notice him at first, for she was half-turned away, her attention caught by something else. Tryggvi waged a quick internal debate on whether he should try to catch her attention or leave her be. He'd just about decided to step away and not be a bother, when suddenly she turned, and her sea-blue eyes found his.

"Good morning!" she said, smiling brightly, and Tryggvi found himself smiling back at her, with hardly a thought.

"Today's the day, isn't it?" she continued cheerfully, but the way she bounced on her toes betrayed her nervousness. "With any luck, we'll break the curse today!"

"I hope so," Tryggvi said, tapping his fingertips on his thigh. He could feel emotions rushing inside him, excitement and fear and hope twining all about each other until he could hardly tell them apart. "I made a promise to someone to bring him back, after all, and I'd prefer not to do that when he's a bear if I can avoid it."

Rósfrída giggled, but her laughter seemed to die far more swiftly than usual. When she spoke again, her voice was still cheerful, but her smile didn't seem to match her eyes.

"You'll take good care of him for me?" she asked. "He's been a very great friend, and I'll miss him when he leaves the mountain."

"I promise to take the very best care of him," Tryggvi replied solemnly, "but there's no need to miss him so soon. It's not like we'll be leaving, you know."

Rósfrída blinked. "But—didn't you just say you have someone waiting for you to bring him back?"

"So I do," Tryggvi said, and laced his hands thoughtfully behind his head. "Unfortunately, I think our father would have our hides if we came home while leaving a very important friend of ours stuck in a mirror. Not exactly princely behavior, that." He grinned and winked at the mirror. "So I suppose there's nothing for it. We'll just stay on the mountain until we get you out of there, simple as that."

The girl stared, mouth hanging open in utter consternation. "Simple?" she finally managed, though it was more of a shriek than a recognizable word. "What do you mean, *simple*? There's no way to get me out—everyone's tried and failed—"

"Not *everyone*," Tryggvi pointed out, still grinning. "I haven't tried yet."

"But you can't—" Rósfrída gasped, rubbing her sleeve across her eyes, her voice cracking. "There's no way—"

"I'll see if there's no way for myself," Tryggvi said firmly, crossing his arms across his chest. "I'll have you know I waited ten years to find a way to help Björn, and I'm not going to give up any sooner where you're concerned."

"I didn't ask you, though," Rósfrída sobbed. "I don't want you to be stuck here worrying about me—"

"I know you didn't ask," he replied, but his voice had gentled, and he reached out towards the mirror, his fingers itching to wipe her tears away. After a moment, he let the hand fall, and clenched his fists against his uselessness. "That's all right. I decided to do it, all by myself. And I know that Björn feels the same way. He cares about you, you know. He has a habit of adopting little siblings and smothering them with brotherly affection.

"And as far as the worrying is concerned," he continued, "I'd be worrying about you even if I was on the other side of the sea, so I'd much rather be doing my worrying here where I can be of use."

Rósfrída had buried her face in her hands, crying great, heaving sobs, and Tryggvi watched her sadly for a long, long moment, desperately grasping for words.

"Of course, if you don't want us to help you, well… then I won't. Mother always says that unless you want to be helped, any sort of help will go wrong. So, if… if you don't want our help, then we'll go home, just as you want. But," he said, and his voice was soft and he didn't dare raise his head and see her face, "I want to help you, very badly. So, I ask you—will you accept our help?"

Rósfrída had finally stopped sobbing; Tryggvi was nearly convinced she'd also stopped breathing; she was so still.

He watched her and felt a breathless coil in his chest wind tighter and tighter, waiting on bated breath for her decree.

Slowly, tentatively, with her hands still clasped over her face, Rósfrída dipped her chin in a nod.

The coil released all at once, and all of Tryggvi's breath rushed out of his lungs in one great sigh. He grinned, feeling suddenly as if there was nothing he couldn't manage.

"Just you wait and see, Rósfrída," he said, putting as much conviction and determination into his voice as he could. "We'll get you out of here soon, right enough."

Rósfrída didn't respond at first; instead, she carefully wiped away all the dampness her tears had left on her cheeks, her head still bowed. Only when she was satisfied did she lift her head.

When she did, she was smiling.

Her cheeks were red and blotchy, her nose was even redder, and small red marks littered the skin beneath her eyes, but somehow all these made her smile even brighter and lovelier than Tryggvi could say.

"I believe you," she said.

Her voice was trembling, the sound thin and reedy, but her eyes burned with a hope she hadn't had in a long, long time.

The sun was still low in the sky when they assembled in the clearing by Eylir's grove, low enough that the grass still sparkled from the scattered diamonds dew had bestowed upon the ground.

The night before, Rósfrída had reported Svanhilda's news to the brothers: namely, that Ingiborg had no knowledge of any weakness they could exploit. So now, there was only one direction in which they could turn.

Svanhilda, with Allvaldi cradled in her arms, had gotten there first, though they were not forced to wait for very long. As soon as Tryggvi and Björn came into view, however, Allvaldi squirmed and slipped his way to the ground and trotted across the grass in order to twine himself about Tryggvi's legs.

Tryggvi let out a laugh and bent down to pet him, burying his fingers in thick golden fur. "What a fine greeting!" he said with a grin. "Did you miss me so much?"

'Don't flatter yourself,' Allvaldi replied without missing a beat, *'It's simply that, after an entire night separated from my glorious presence, I just happened to notice that there is an appalling lack of ME on your clothes.'*

"Ah." Tryggvi looked down at the long golden furs that had already begun to migrate onto his trousers. "That's more like it."

"Are you ready?" Svanhilda called.

Tryggvi obligingly scooped up Allvaldi onto his shoulder. "So you don't miss out blessing my tunic with your 'glorious presence'."

'Excellent thinking. I see my training is beginning to take effect at last.'

Tryggvi rolled his eyes, ignoring the amused stare from the bear that was his brother, and they followed Svanhilda into the grove.

Flosi was waiting just inside, sitting on a low-hanging branch, though he leapt down when he saw them coming. "Follow me," he said, gesturing over his shoulder. "My father is this way."

All three followed after him silently, and Svanhilda pulled her mirror from her purse for Rósfrída, now that her arms were empty of the great, all-encompassing burden that is a cat.

Flosi walked confidently through the twisting paths of the grove before coming to an abrupt stop in front of a small clearing in the center.

The first thing Tryggvi noticed was not Flosi's father, but the great boar with fur the color of liquid gold that was lying down at the foot a nearby tree, fast asleep.

Tryggvi stared at it, long and hard, then quickly glanced at his companions, to see if they were seeing the same thing that he was.

Considering Björn's wide eyes, Svanhilda's pale face, and Rósfrída's excited expression in the mirror, he definitely wasn't imagining it.

Every child in that land knew of the great Golden Boar of the woods. He featured in a hundred tales, for such a magnificent creature was worthy only to be the steed of an equally worthy personage.

Namely: Freyvid Alfrikr, King of the Elves.

Allvaldi gracefully slipped down from Tryggvi's shoulder, and trotted across the clearing, tail waving as high and proudly as a banner. The cat preceded to take a seat at the base of a stump and bat plaintively at the boot of the man sitting upon a rock in the center of the clearing.

The man—or rather, elf—was tall and slender with hair as golden as the sun, which fell nearly to the ground, and an equally golden, neatly trimmed beard. On his head was a crown of emeralds carved like the leaves of ash tree, set on a branch of gold. His clothes were as green as summer, and from his shoulders flowed a cloak woven of ivy and flowering vines.

He reached down and bestowed several pets upon Allvaldi's head. Allvaldi purred loudly enough to be heard across the clearing.

After a long moment, Freyvid Alfrikr looked up, and he smiled, and Tryggvi thought that not even the sun could compare to the brightness and warmth of that expression.

"Svanhilda and Rósfrída, daughters of Ingiborg and Kiúli, I wish to thank you," he said, his voice rich and warm, full of kindness. "My son Eylir's grove is quite isolated upon this mountain, and thus he is often away from his brothers and sisters. Thank you for giving him friends."

"Of course!" Rósfrída exclaimed, forgetting that the King could not hear her—though, by the way his green eyes focused on the mirror in Svanhilda's hand, perhaps he could.

"We were glad to!" Svanhilda said. "He was very kind to us when we first met him, and we were glad to return the favor with company."

King Freyvid nodded, satisfied, then swept his gaze over them all.

"My son Flosi tells me you have a question to ask me—a question regarding a curse."

Björn took a deep breath and stepped forward, bowing his head slightly. "Yes. Long ago, this torque was placed around my neck by a dwarven smith, binding me to this form."

"As long as that dwarf's power remains connected to this torque, there is no way to remove it," Flosi explained, suddenly stepping forward. "But I do not know of a method to do so, and those I know who might know the answer—" he gestured helplessly.

"Rather elusive, as usual, I deem," Alfrikr hummed, amused. "Yes, I can see why you came to me."

"So?" Tryggvi asked, heart in his throat. "Is there a way?"

The King observed them silently for a moment: Björn, stiff as a statue; Tryggvi with wide eyes and clenched fists; Svanhilda clutching Rósfrída's mirror close to her heart.

Flosi, his son, with a painful hope in his gaze.

"I think…" King Freyvid said slowly, "you are not inclined to use such knowledge for ill. Swear to me that this will be so, and I shall tell you."

Four voices spoke as one. "I swear!"

Amusement quirked the corner of the King's mouth. "Very well, I shall tell you. It did not use to be a secret, but dwarves do not live as long as my people, and there are none now alive who remember the way it used to be—when dwarves and elves and men all dwelt near each other, and there was great friendship between the three kindreds. But that is long forgotten by all save the elves, I am afraid, and a great many secrets have been forgotten as well. Or," his eyes twinkled, "nearly so."

"The secret," he announced, with a grand sweep of his arm, "is that both elves and dwarves have the same weakness: our power is sealed within our skin, and there is only one conduit with which it can escape into the air, so we can use it and shape it."

There was a long moment of confused silence, and the King's amused expression transformed into a full smile.

"Have you never wondered why elves and dwarf-women wear their hair long, and dwarven men do not trim their beards?"

CHAPTER 6

pon delivering his message, the Elven King had swiftly mounted his great boar and ridden off into the woods.

Now, Tryggvi laid sprawled on his back in the grass of the clearing, staring up at the sky and trying to figure out how it had come to this. "I can't believe the answer is to cut off his beard."

"It's not exactly what I've been imagining for the past decade," Björn agreed with a grunt.

"How are we even supposed to get close enough to cut off his beard?" Rósfrída asked.

A sudden thought struck Tryggvi, and he sat up abruptly. "Forget the beard for a moment; don't we need to find whoever it is that did this in the first place? After all, we can't cut off a beard if there's no beard to cut off."

"An excellent question," Flosi remarked from his perch in a nearby tree. He plucked idly at the strings of his lap harp, staring off into the middle distance. "Just who on earth would have the motivation to do such a thing to an innocent child?"

The words fell into the clearing like stones dropped from on high into a still pond, sending ripples careening towards the shore.

Tryggvi turned slowly towards Flosi, eyes narrowed. "You know something," he said flatly.

"I *know* nothing," Flosi countered. "I simply have a guess."

"And that is?" Svanhilda said quietly.

Allvaldi rose from the stone in the center of the clearing where he had been soaking up the sun, and slunk his way across the clearing to the young woman, sliding his way into her lap. Her hand reached up and began to stroke his back, though the movement was listless and detached.

Flosi eyed her curiously, and one eyebrow rose as his mouth twisted into a bitter smile. "Perhaps," he said, gently, "you have guessed something yourself?"

Tryggvi's, Björn's, and Rósfrída's gazes all snapped toward Svanhilda.

"You know who it is, Svana?" Rósfrída gasped.

Björn stared at her for a long moment, then turned his head away, settling his chin on his paws and closing his eyes.

Tryggvi felt something unpleasant curdle in his gut. He wasn't entirely sure what was going on, so he decided to get the answers from the most likely culprit.

He stood up and crossed his arms over his chest, narrowing his gaze on the elven bard perched in the tree, like some strange, overlarge songbird. "What I want to know at the moment, is why exactly someone like you—a son of the King of the Elves—is poking his nose into our business?" He paused for a second, then continued hastily. "Not that we aren't grateful for your help; but why do you seem so determined to meddle? What are you even doing here in the first place?"

Flosi plucked several notes on his harp. "…Would you believe I was keeping my baby brother company?"

"Somehow," Svanhilda said, her voice still somewhat quiet and subdued, "I do not think that was the sole basis of your motivation."

The bard pressed his lips together, his fingers stilling on the strings. After a long, long moment he spoke.

"Ten years ago, someone sent me here to keep an eye on Alvíss' mirror in the wake of his death. Mirrors embedded with power can be extremely dangerous if not handled carefully, and the circumstances of your Grandfather's death… concerned my friend greatly. We were worried it would have an adverse effect on the mirror, and if not handled properly… well. Bad things would happen."

Tryggvi swallowed. He'd heard tales of dark mirrors, told by the bards before the fire during the long dark of winter. "How bad?"

Flosi grinned darkly. "Very."

"Well…" Tryggvi bit his lip. "That seems reasonable, but still…

who sent you in the first place?"

The bard hummed. He played one note, a low, ringing sound. "Does the name 'The Wanderer' ring any bells?"

Utter silence descended upon the clearing.

"Oh." Tryggvi finally managed to squeak out.

"*Oh*, indeed," Flosi repeated, fingers moving towards the strings of his harp—but they fell, limp and soundless, back into his lap.

"I guarded the mirror for three years and kept it safe—but I failed to consider certain possibilities, and a little girl suffered for my mistake. I…" He let out a long, shuddering sigh. "I wish to fix two things: first, the injustice that led to Björn's curse; and secondly, to atone for my foolish mistake and free Rósfrída. So that's why I'm 'meddling', as you called it."

Flosi shrugged, leaning his head back against the trunk of his tree and closing his eyes. "I hope that, with this business, everything might finally be put to rights."

There was a stunned silence, one which no one dared to break.

No one, that is, except Rósfrída.

Her voice was quiet; Tryggvi could hardly believe Flosi could hear her from so far away, but the bard's unwavering attention was fixed on the small mirror Svanhilda still held in one hand, despite his eyes being closed.

"I don't blame you, Master Bard," she said, hands clasped against her heart. "I'm sure you did your best. And I probably shouldn't have been poking around in strange caves by myself. If you are to bear any blame, I must too." She shot a quick glare at Svanhilda. "My sister would like to think it's her fault, but she's wrong."

Svanhilda smiled faintly at this, and Allvaldi rumbled a purr beneath her hand.

"A-anyway," Rósfrída continued, her voice slowly but surely gaining strength and volume, "while I appreciate your desire to help, please don't blame yourself any more."

"But, I cannot express how sorry I am—"

"You don't need to, though," she replied, and smiled. "I know… and I forgive you, and that is all that needs to be said."

Flosi looked at her for a long, long moment, then finally dipped his head in a deep bow, a faint smile on his face. "…Thank you. Let it be as you said, then, my lady."

"Good!" Rósfrída nodded to herself, well pleased, and Tryggvi smiled fondly at the mirror, retaking his seat upon the grass.

Björn shuffled a little closer and whispered, "What exactly just happened?"

"I'll tell you later," his brother hissed back, and Björn grumbled and subsided.

"What I want to know," Tryggvi spoke into the ensuing silence—

'You mean, besides all the other things you wanted to know in the last hour or so?' Allvaldi pointed out.

"Yes, thank you, Allvaldi," Tryggvi groaned with a roll of his eye. "What I meant, was, what I'm still curious about is what defeating the dwarf that cursed Björn has to do with freeing Rósfrída."

"Ah," Flosi said. "Well." He tapped his fingers on the pillar of his lap harp. "You see, the reason my protection was so necessary was that there is a certain, particularly determined person who wishes to get inside the vault, and he may or may not be in possession of the key."

"Let me guess," Tryggvi said. "This particularly determined person wouldn't happen to be the dwarf that cursed Björn?"

Flosi nodded.

"Well, then!" Tryggvi shot up to his feet again. "What's stopping us? We can kill two birds with one stone if we capture this fellow and cut off his beard!"

'You still don't know who it is,' Allvaldi pointed out.

"Well, neither do you."

'True, but I, personally, do not happen to harbor a crush on the pretty young woman trapped inside the mirror, so for me, it is a moot point. You, on the other hand—'

Tryggvi's mouth flapped soundlessly. Allvaldi had sufficiently managed to distract him enough that it was a minute before he noticed Björn was speaking to the bard.

"Your wards scared the would-be thief away, didn't they?" the bear asked, and Flosi nodded.

"I owe you a great debt, then," Björn said solemnly. "He was spooked enough that he didn't dare go near the place, which made my duty of guarding the vault much easier. I was even able to slip off and say what were supposed to be final goodbyes."

"You owe me nothing; I was glad to be of help," Flosi said, then raised an eyebrow, amused. "But—supposed?"

"I have a little brother who is rather stubborn."

Flosi laughed. "Brothers and sisters are a gift from Highest Heaven, are they not?"

"So they are," Björn concurred, but his voice was low and solemn.

Svanhilda flinched.

"All this is well and good," Tryggvi cut in, desperately trying to avoid Allvaldi's accusation, "but we still don't have an answer about whom we're supposed to catch." He pointed at the bard. "Flosi knows, or guesses, or whatever, but doesn't want to tell us—"

"It's not my place," Flosi put in quietly.

Tryggvi raised an eyebrow at that, before pointing at Björn. "Björn clearly knows, but he can't tell us, I'm guessing because of the curse—" The bear nodded once, sharply, and Tryggvi nodded in return. "As I thought."

He turned to face Svanhilda, and dropped his hand, tilting his head to one side in confusion. "And... Svanhilda, what do you know?"

Svanhilda shut her eyes tightly, her fingers curling into a fist on top of Allvaldi's back. "I—" She choked, words failing her.

"Svana," Rósfrída said, slowly, a terrible guess in her voice, "Does... does it have to do with Grandfather's death?"

Svana sucked in a breath.

Oh.

Tryggvi had forgotten; not only had Ásbjörn gone missing, but also his tutor—the smith, Alvíss—and his partner and brother, Althjóf.

But... a sudden thought began to cross Tryggvi's mind; a thought that Rósfrída was starting to form herself.

Ásbjörn had survived the accident—in the form of a bear with a cursed torque around his neck.

A cold fist began to clutch at Tryggvi's insides—and if this was how *he* felt, how much more Rósfrída and Svanhilda—

For, if Ásbjörn had survived, who was to say one of the others had not survived? Who was to say there was even an accident, at all?

What was it that Allvaldi had said—was it yesterday? It felt like a month ago…

'If there is no obvious gap in a strong gate, I would suspect the gate-keeper if an enemy sneaks through.'

If Allvaldi turned out to be right, Tryggvi would never hear the end of it.

"Björn…" Tryggvi said, slowly, "can you tell me—is Master Alvíss dead?"

Björn turned his head away. "…Yes."

"And…" Tryggvi swallowed hard. "His brother—"

Björn shut his eyes and shook his head.

Rósfrída cried out, clapping her hands over her mouth. Svanhilda shrank in on herself, shoulders hunching and head bowed.

Tryggvi sucked in a breath and let it out slowly. "How…" he swallowed hard and forced the words out of his throat. "How are you even still alive?"

Björn wouldn't turn to face him, but Tryggvi could see the way the bear's sides heaved a heavy breath; could see the pain and sorrow in the hunch of his shoulders.

"It was an accident," Björn said, his voice flat. "They were arguing, and Althjóf grew angry, and he snatched up one of their hammers and—" he cut off, shaking his head once. "I ran, but it was raining, and I slipped and fell and hit my head. I suppose he lost his nerve. After all, he hadn't intended to kill Alvíss; he couldn't bring himself to kill another so soon. But he couldn't have me escaping and telling everyone, so he took the pelt and the torque and placed them on me while I slept. When I woke up again, he was gone with a sack full of gold and jewels and precious things, and I was… like this."

He paused for a second, and when next he spoke, there was a note of grim satisfaction in his voice. "It backfired on him, though, for when he returned later to steal more gold… *well.* A bear makes a more formidable guard than a lad of thirteen summers. He never laid his hands on the gold again; but neither could anyone else, for he took the key, as Flosi said."

Well, there it was. The answers Tryggvi had wished for, for ten long years—but it was a bitter draught, indeed. "So…" he said slowly, digging a hand into his hair, "we know how to stop the curse, and we know who to stop now—but how, in all the mountains, are we supposed to pull this off?"

The words hung in the air, and Tryggvi's gaze bounced around the clearing, desperately hoping someone had answers, as he certainly did not.

To everyone's surprise, it was Svanhilda who spoke into the silence.

"I have a plan."

>>*<< · >>*<< · >>*<<

Flosi's fingers danced over the strings of his harp, his brow furrowed in concentration. Finally, he let his fingers fall and he wiped sweat away from his forehead, leaning back from his harp with a sigh.

"There," he said. "My wards and protections are down."

"Will this even work?" Rósfrída asked nervously from the vault's entrance.

"I'm as certain as I can be," Björn huffed. "He was furious when I denied him access to the vault before, and I know he's been lurking on this mountain ever since, waiting for a chance to 'reclaim' the treasure. Trust me; he'll notice when the wards vanish, and he'll come running."

Flosi tipped his head to one side thoughtfully. "And he won't think it's a trap?"

"I doubt it," Svanhilda said quietly. "Uncle, from what I remember, was always convinced of the greatness of his own intelligence and skill. That someone might try to trick him would probably never cross his mind."

Flosi nodded, then clapped his hands. "Right! Well then, I'll join Tryggvi as he prepares for part two of the plan. The two of you should go hide yourselves." With that, he ducked out of the cave, leaving Svanhilda and Björn alone.

"Will you be all right?" the bear asked Svanhilda softly.

151

She swallowed hard, but smiled as she patted the cord that hung from her belt, from which dangled a pair of iron shears. "I have my shears right here with me. I'll be fine!"

Björn nodded and butted his head against her shoulder. "Be careful," he rumbled quietly.

Svanhilda wrapped her arms around his neck in return, burying her face in the soft fur. "Of course; as long as you promise to do the same."

A great, rumbling chuckle filled the room, and Björn reached up with one paw and hugged her back as gently as he could. "I promise."

"Svana…" Rósfrída's voice was like a splash of cold water on the face of someone fast asleep, jerking Svanhilda back into awareness, her heart beating frantically. She snapped her head around to face the mirror.

Rósfrída's eyes were wide, and her face was pale as she tugged nervously at the end of her braid, but her jaw was set with determination. "I just heard from Tryggvi. He said one of the birds spotted a dwarf climbing the mountain, heading this way!"

Svanhilda swallowed and stepped back from Björn, straightening her shoulders and lifting her chin.

"We had better hide," Björn cautioned.

Svanhilda nodded sharply. "Right."

Björn stepped away and turned to the mirror—it was really the only place someone his size could hide, and he'd be on hand in case he was needed.

Svanhilda, however, was much smaller, and no one wanted to risk her trying to hide in the mirror. Instead, she darted over to the great pile of furs that made up Björn's bed and quickly burrowed into it. She pulled fur after fur over her and squirmed carefully around, so she lay on her belly, facing the door. She was completely covered, a thick, warm weight pressing her down, shielded from anyone's notice. Even if Althjóf paid attention to the pile of furs in the corner, he wouldn't notice anything amiss.

Now… all they had to do was wait.

Waiting is not the most pleasant of experiences. Time stretched on and on, each moment dragging across the ground like a slug.

Every one of Svanhilda's breaths rasped loudly in her ears and scraped dryly against her throat, and each heartbeat echoed like a drum in her chest. She dug her fingers into the fur beneath her and squeezed, breathing in and out, trying to force her heartbeat to calm.

Just as she managed to get her heart to stop pounding in her ears, a shadow fell across the threshold of the cave.

Svanhilda went rigid, her knuckles whitening as her grip on the fur redoubled.

It had been a decade since she had seen her great-uncle Althjóf, and the years had not been kind. He was wizened and dirty; his once neat, dark beard was streaked with gray and matted, and his eyes gleamed greedily. He was a shell of his former self; all the pride of a craftsman had deserted him, and the only thing left to fill the void within himself was the lust for rich and glorious things.

Svanhilda had suspected for a long, long time the secrets surrounding her grandfather's death and Ásbjörn's curse, but that did not make the truth any easier to bear.

Althjóf had never been the most pleasant company and had had little time for children. Still, he had been her grandfather's brother, and Alvíss had loved him; he had been family. So, Svanhilda had loved him, too, and mourned him when he died.

Except—he was not dead. He was here; and he was responsible for the sorrows of both her best friend and her little sister.

Svanhilda was not her uncle. She loved Rósfrída with all her heart, and she would not let his selfishness hurt anyone she cared about any longer.

Althjóf stumbled forward toward the mirror-door, one of his hands already outstretched and grasping. "At last," he mumbled, so quietly Svanhilda could barely understand him. "It's been so long, but that meddling elf has finally left, and taken that dog of a prince with him. I knew this day would come—all my waiting has been worth it!"

His free hand fumbled at his belt, pulling out a bronze key that had been tied to a string. Svanhilda's heart leapt to her throat—there it was. The signal.

Althjóf lifted the key. At the very same moment, Björn leapt out of the mirror, teeth bared. The dwarf fell back with a shout, ducking underneath the bear's outstretched paws by sheer luck, and scrambled to his feet, fleeing towards the exit.

No matter, they were prepared.

"Tryggvi! Now!" Rósfríða called out, and Tryggvi and Flosi charged into the cave.

They were not alone.

The elves love the creatures of the forest and know their voices, and the animals love them in return. So Tryggvi and Flosi had gone to them and asked for help, and help they got.

At their heels swarmed a horde of creatures, streaming into the cave, and as one they charged at Althjóf. There were lynxes, forest cats, polecats, even a wolverine, and at their head ran Allvaldi, his golden tail streaming behind him as proudly as a king's banner.

They swarmed over the dwarf like a wave crashing onto the shore and bore him to the ground. Althjóf screamed and fought, limbs flailing wildly, and yet not a single creature fought back; all their focus was kept on swarming him and keeping him down.

Svanhilda burst out from underneath the furs, sprinted across the room, wading fearlessly through the milling horde of animals, and seized ahold of Althjóf's beard, pulling it into the air.

The dwarf's eyes widened, fear shining in them like the eyes of a cornered animal lit by torchlight.

With a swift movement of her arm, she brought her shears to bear and snipped three times, as close to the chin as she dared.

With the last snip of the shears, Althjóf's head fell back against the floor. He screamed with the sudden confusion of a terrible fear and loss.

To have something be a part of you all your life, and to suddenly have that ripped away, is like losing a sense; it leaves you hollow and groping, helpless for something you can no longer reach. Althjóf's screams turned to howls of rage, and he tried to snatch at Svanhilda and pull her down.

Svanhilda scampered away just in time, retreating safely to Björn's side. She stared down at the writhing form of her great uncle, who was almost entirely submerged beneath the sea of woodland creatures, and she pitied him—he'd been warned what devastation his greed would bring, but he had failed to heed his brother's words.

Instead, he'd repaid Alvíss' care with violence. Even now, he struck out angrily at those around him.

She shuddered and buried her face in the fur of Björn's shoulder.

Tryggvi drew his sword and thrust it skyward like a commander marshaling an army. "Althjóf the Kin-slayer!" he bellowed, and at the sound of his voice, all the animals froze, silent and unmoving. Althjóf's voice cut off abruptly at the address, and he lay there beneath the horde of creatures, tense and waiting.

"I do not wish to kill you, Master Althjóf," Tryggvi said, gray eyes narrowing coldly down at the pathetic lump of dwarf upon the floor. "There has been enough blood and pain, hurt and hate on this mountain already. But neither will I let you hurt anyone else; not if it is within my power to stop it. So here is what I offer you: leave this mountain, this country, and go far away, to a place where you will be no harm to anyone who knew you once—and no more harm will come to you. I deem the misery of being separated from your treasure will be a great punishment, but it is preferable to losing your life. What say you?"

"And don't think you can sneak back into this land once you leave," Flosi added with an idle strum of his harp, his voice pleasant but his eyes cold. "I will know if you return, and I'll deal with you myself."

There was a long silence before Althjóf stirred at last. When he spoke, his voice was raspy and raw from his screams. "How noble," he scoffed. "Do you think yourself righteous, or are you simply a coward, a human whelp still wet behind the ears, afraid to have blood on his hands?"

"No," Tryggvi said calmly. "I am merely a man who has a brother that he cherishes, and if Alvíss was even half the man tales have named him, he would not want his little brother slain in his name."

Althjóf flinched violently at the sound of his brother's name, scowling. After a moment he spoke, his tone angry and begrudging. "Call off your vermin; I submit to your terms."

Tryggvi's shoulders relaxed, and he returned his sword to his sheath. "Thank you, everyone. You can return home, now."

Within moments, the animals had scampered and slunk from the room, leaving only Allvaldi, who hissed one last time at Althjóf before retreating to Tryggvi's side.

Slowly, Althjóf stumbled to his feet and staggered towards the entrance to the cave, bruised and beaten after being swarmed by several score animals.

Something was nagging at Svanhilda however, and Althjóf had hardly gone three steps before it hit her like a thunderbolt.

"Wait, uncle!" she cried out, and ran forward, darting in front of him with her hand outstretched. "Before you go, you have to give us the key to the vault. It's not yours to keep."

Althjóf stared up at her, at this girl with eyes that reminded him of his brother, and he remembered that she had been the one to seize his beard and cut it away. She had tossed it aside like trash, and left him feeling hollow and empty and blind, and rage for all the perceived indignities and injustices that he had suffered that day—assault and thievery, his beard cut, banishment and pity and mercy—swelled up within his heart and mind like a black tide.

Rósfrída had had a very little role in the plan, as she could not step foot beyond the mirror. Instead, she'd helped where she could—helping the two groups communicate and helping the pieces of the plan to move together smoothly. But once everything was in place, there was no more use for Rósfrída. She'd been stuck inside her little room, watching everyone else fight for her and Björn's freedom while she stood there, helpless. So she watched, and waited, trying to ignore the uselessness grating at her heart.

But because she was forced to stand there and watch, she was the only one who saw the quick movement of Althjóf's arm; saw the shine of a blade being unsheathed.

"SVANA! LOOK OUT!"

Tryggvi and Flosi were on the other side of the cave, too far away to be any help. Svanhilda tried to get away, but the dagger was already in motion.

Time is a fickle thing. Hours of happiness can seem but like a moment passed, while the most dreadful second can stretch into an eternity of hell. For one breathless, terrible moment, Rósfrída was trapped within this eternity, as she realized there was no one else to hear her, no one to help. There was no hope left.

In that dreadful moment, Rósfrída could not remember that there is *always* hope.

In the Highest Heaven is the Lea of Flame, and the Lea of Flame is filled with a spirit of mercy. It reached out and tweaked the threads that fate had spun—and in that dreadful moment, Björn's ears were opened.

Svanhilda was knocked to one side when the entire bulk of a great white bear slammed into her. Althjóf's knife sank into Björn's foreleg, but it did little to protect the dwarf from the large, clawed paw that came swinging at his head in the next moment.

There was a sickening thunk and crack and Althjóf was tossed to one side. He crumpled onto the stone and lay still, like a discarded rag thrown upon the ground.

There was a stunned silence.

Svanhilda sat up from where she was sprawled on the ground, one hand rising to her mouth in shock. "Is… is he…?"

They all stared at the body, yet no one seemed able to step forward and check.

Luckily for them, Allvaldi was made of sterner stuff. He trotted forward, sniffed once or twice, and lashed his tail. *Definitely dead. Good riddance, too.'*

Tryggvi let out a sigh, though he couldn't quite tell if it was from relief or simply exhaustion. "Thank you, Allvaldi."

Allvaldi didn't answer at first, as he had busied himself with biting through the string attached to the key. In a minute it was free, and Allvaldi picked it up and trotted over to his human, depositing it at Tryggvi's feet as delicately as if it were a mouse's corpse.

'Of course. After all, you lot would be absolutely hopeless without me.'

Tryggvi laughed softly, and bent over to retrieve the key, making sure to give the cat several good scratches first. "So we would, my friend. So we would."

Then he picked up the key and turned to face his brother—just in time to see Björn disappear inside the mirror.

A girl and a bear stood face to face in a room full of treasure with mirrors for walls, just as they once did, seven long years before.

"You heard me," Rósfrída whispered, her eyes wide with shock, tears still streaming down her cheeks, as if the fact that Svanhilda was fine—that it was Althjóf who had died instead—hadn't quite sunk in yet.

"So I did," Björn said, and nudged her shoulder with his nose.

"How, though? You've never heard me before—"

"I think," Björn said, cutting her off gently, "that there are things in this world that we may never understand; all we can do is simply rejoice that it did."

Rósfrída contemplated this for a moment, nodded, and then flung her arms around the bear's neck.

"Thank you for saving Svana."

"It was my pleasure," he rumbled. "Now... I believe I owe you something."

Rósfrída blinked in surprise, and she stepped back, wiping her nose and sniffling. "You do? What's that?"

"A long time ago, I promised you a ride out of this room," Björn said, and smiled as best as a bear can. "I believe it's about time I fulfilled that promise."

>>*<< · >>*<< · >>*<<

"Here," Tryggvi said, pressing the key into Svanhilda's hand. It was made of bronze, with a bow that had been carved in the shape of a bear inside a ring. "I believe you had best do the honors."

Svanhilda grasped the key, squeezing tightly to prevent them from shaking over-much. She took a deep breath and faced the mirror.

She could see Rósfrída in her reflection, even now—though it was hazy and faint, as Rósfrída was clearly not attending to the world outside the mirror.

This mirror had taken something very precious, a long time ago.

Svanhilda squared her shoulders and raised her chin.

Now the time had come to get it back.

She reached out and pressed the key to the mirror's glass. In the next moment, the surface rippled and a black nose appeared.

Svanhilda took several steps back to give Björn room, and watched as first a white head emerged, followed by broad shoulders, and then—a brilliant smile and hair the color of rowan's berries, all belonging to the girl perched triumphantly on the back of a great white bear.

"Hey, Svana," Rósfrída said, smiling even brighter, "I guess you're back to your boring old reflection now, huh?"

Her sister opened her mouth to retort, but all that came out was a sob. Then Rósfrída tumbled off the bear's back and into Svanhilda's arms, and for the first time in seven years Svanhilda hugged her little sister tight.

Björn smiled at the pair before turning to Tryggvi. "Well," he rumbled, "now *that* has been done, I don't suppose you'd like to help me take this blasted thing off? It's rather hot in the summer, you know."

Tryggvi laughed and reached for the torque. "Well, if you insist, big brother."

With a simple twist, the silver torque was off and discarded on the ground, and Flosi obligingly kicked it aside. It rolled across the ground and lay against the wall, its only remaining purpose to gather dust and tarnish.

Tryggvi forgot all about it however, for Björn gave himself a mighty shake—and then it was like watching a snake shed its skin. White fur puddled on the floor, and Ásbjörn stood before him, smiling down at Tryggvi. He was clad in rags, and his hair had grown long, and he looked nothing like the boy Tryggvi remembered—yet he'd recognize him in a heartbeat.

"Wanderer's staff, you have a beard!" Tryggvi gasped.

Ásbjörn blinked. "Wait, I do?"

He began to reach up to feel for himself, but a sudden, sharp pain in his arm made his stop, wincing.

Tryggvi saw his brief look of pain and glanced down at his brother's arm, only to have his eyes shoot wide open from shock.

"And a wound in your arm!"

Ásbjörn stared down at his arm, blinking in confusion. There was, indeed, a bleeding wound on his arm—left by Althjóf's knife.

"Ooooh. I had forgotten about that."

The mention of a wound was enough to pull Svanhilda from hugging her little sister and awaken the furious she-bear that slept inside. "What's all this about a wound?" she snapped, hands on her hips.

Tryggvi pointed at his brother. "Ásbjörn got stabbed in the arm!"

"Snitch!" Ásbjörn hissed. Tryggvi stuck out his tongue at him.

Svanhilda's attention, however, was fixed on the wound as she took Ásbjörn's arm and frowned down at it with a shake of her head. "Honestly! How could you not notice there was a wound in your arm?"

"Well, until about three minutes ago, I was a bear, and that wound isn't very big compared to a bear's leg. So, I didn't pay it much attention?"

Svanhilda took his other hand and began to lead him out of the cave, still frowning fiercely. "It's still a wound! Which is *bleeding*! You should have been paying attention to it!"

Rósfrída and Tryggvi looked at each other, smiled, and followed their siblings out into the light, Flosi and Allvaldi trailing behind.

Althjóf's body was left on the floor of the cave, alone in the dark; there was no one there to mourn him.

CHAPTER 7

Once Björn's wound had been bandaged, they all sat silently by the edge of the pool fed by the waterfall, and the reality of what had happened—what they had just done—sank into them.

Rósfrída was free; Björn had regained his true form.

Althjóf was dead.

No one, it seemed, really knew what to say.

Rósfrída was not a creature made for silence, however, so after a while she stirred herself and spoke. "So, I've been wondering…"

Tryggvi hummed, eyes closed as he lay on the shore and basked in the warmth of the sun. Rósfrída took this as the encouragement it was meant to be and continued, "How on earth was Allvaldi able to hear and see me?"

Tryggvi sat up. "Huh. I didn't think of that." He turned to his cat, who was sprawled out and lounging upon the sun-warmed surface of a nearby boulder. "How could you see Rósfrída, Allvaldi?"

Allvaldi flicked his tail. *'A fool is he who gives away his secrets so carelessly.'*

Tryggvi repeated this for the benefit of the non-elves in the company. Ásbjörn laughed.

"By which Master Allvaldi means he doesn't know but doesn't want to admit it."

The cat decided not to dignify this with a reply and turned his back on Ásbjörn with a sniff.

"Whether or not Allvaldi knows the answer, I might have one for you," Flosi said from his perch in a nearby tree.

Rósfrída perked up, always excited to learn something new. "What's that, Master Flosi?"

"Allvaldi, as I am sure you are aware," Flosi began, plucking a tune out on the strings of his harp, "is an elf-cat, and as such is sensitive to the rhythms of power in the world. Also, he has spent his life since kitten-hood near that little amber stone of Tryggvi's— an eye that allows the bearer to see clearly. It's a particularly powerful specimen—" An amused smile spread across his face. "I suppose you could say that even I, in all my wanderings, have only once found its match."

Tryggvi stared down at the stone in wonder, rolling it between his fingers and watching the sun gleam golden in its amber depths.

"All that aside," Flosi added, tipping his head to one side as he swept his gaze over them all, "what exactly is the plan now?"

"Well…" Ásbjörn coughed, scratching thoughtfully at his new beard. "We need to bury Althjóf, first."

Why should we bother? He's not fit for ravens to feast on—' Allvaldi began, but Tryggvi smoothly reached over and flicked his nose.

Feeling betrayed, Allvaldi slunk off to enjoy the company of the only one who truly appreciated him—namely, himself. He ran up the nearest tree and lounged on a high branch, judgmentally staring down at the unappreciative peasants below.

"I'll send a message to his people," Flosi said solemnly, "so they can bury him in whatever manner seems best to them. But, putting that gloomy subject aside, I'm far more curious about what you four shall be doing."

"Going home," Ásbjörn said, promptly, and reached out to ruffle Tryggvi's hair. Tryggvi didn't even try to duck away, as he might have as a child. "I made a promise to someone a long time ago, and it seems I'm a bit late."

Tryggvi choked on a laugh and slugged Ásbjörn in the side. Ásbjörn returned this with an affectionate headlock, and it may have escalated if Svanhilda hadn't spoken up.

"I do hope you won't be fighting each other with that arm of yours, Björn."

Ásbjörn froze and slowly slipped away from Tryggvi, who shot him a triumphant smirk. "Ah, of-of course not."

"I thought so," Svanhilda said primly, but then she smiled.

It was a very lovely smile, and it prompted Ásbjörn to drag up some words that had been lurking in the back of his mind for a very, very long time.

"I'll miss you," he began, swallowing hard.

"I'll miss you, too," she said, her smile becoming softer and gentler.

Ásbjörn shifted awkwardly. "You don't *have* to miss me, you know."

"Oh, no?" Svanhilda tilted her head to one side, her smile coy but her eyes shining. "And what makes you say that?"

"Well.." Björn said, picking his words carefully, "if it is your will, my lady, I would be honored to have you—"

"You can't ask her that," Rósfrída cut in primly. "Mama says you have to wait until you talk to Father before you get anyone's consent."

There was a moment of silence in which Björn's eyebrows arched heavenward, broken abruptly by a screech.

"RÓSFRÍDA!"

Svanhilda's face was now of a color to match the rowans her sister was named after. "You—you heard that?"

"You keep your mirror in your purse," Rósfrída retorted with a grin. "I couldn't help but hear, really."

Svanhilda's mouth opened and closed several times, like a landed fish gasping for air. Björn, however, reached out and took her hand in his. "Then, I simply shall have to wait. When your father returns, may I speak with you then?"

The embarrassed flush on Svanhilda's cheeks softened into a gentle glow, and she smiled down at his hand. "I would like that very much."

She glanced back up at him, staring into his eyes, and the pair of them might have become quite lost if Rósfrída hadn't intervened. She nudged Svanhilda with her shoulder, giggling. "Now, now, Svana. You can't go off and get married; it's not fair!"

"Oh, really?" Svanhilda turned and arched an eyebrow at her. "And why is that?"

"Because!" Rósfrída grinned. "Don't you remember? Mama

made us promise to share everything, and you can't very well share a suitor!" She shook her head. "I'm sorry, Svana, but there's just no way you can accept this."

Svanhilda sighed and lifted her eyes to heaven, and Ásbjörn coughed loudly, covering his mouth with a fist. Flosi didn't even bother to hide his laughter.

"Ah, well, I might have a solution for that," Tryggvi drawled, his voice thoughtful.

Rósfrída laughed, spreading her hands wide in mock supplication. "If you do, please share it, for my sister's sake!"

"Oh yes, please, save me," Svanhilda said dryly.

"Well…" Tryggvi said. "I happen to be Ásbjörn's brother, so we're basically the same person."

Ásbjörn snorted. Tryggvi wrinkled his nose at his brother before turning his attention back to Rósfrída with a sunny smile. "If I court you, would that satisfy the sharing requirement?"

Rósfrída's eyes went very wide, and she glanced down at her lap, furiously twisting the end of her braid. She coughed twice, hunching her shoulders to hide the blood rushing to her ears. "I… suppose that's an acceptable solution."

"So?" Tryggvi leaned a little closer, trying to get a look at her bowed face. "What do you say, my lady Rósfrída?"

"W-well," she stuttered, quickly glancing to one side, "it's not like I can decide anything before Father gets back either, but…" She peeked back at him shyly, before mustering herself and raising her chin. "I guess I'll think about it."

Tryggvi's grin was brighter than the sun, and he bowed. "I'm very grateful… for my brother's sake, of course."

"Of course," Rósfrída nodded, "and for my sister's."

Then they burst into laughter, Svanhilda and Ásbjörn joining in; the ringing notes of their mirth blending with the music of the waterfall.

Allvaldi looked down at the four seated on the ground, and huffed, giving his eyes a mighty roll. *'Idiots. They're all idiots.'* He huffed again, with a flick of his tail and softening of his green eyes. *'Still, my idiots they are, and so they shall remain.'*

Flosi laughed quietly in his tree, his smile wide even if his eyes were wistful, and he quietly began to pluck out a new song, a song of beginnings.

For the first time in a great many years, all at last was well with the world.

>>*<< · >>*<< · >>*<<

"Where in the world are we? Where did you bring me?" a man snapped, scrabbling to find his balance as he suddenly appeared in the branches of a tree. Once he'd managed to stabilize himself, he lifted his head and let himself feel the wind. He blinked.

"Is this the Northland? I'm not supposed to be here for several months yet! Why did you bring me here?"

His companion lounged gracefully against the tree trunk on a neighboring branch, an eyebrow arched imperiously. "You know, Funi, one would expect from your history you'd be grateful to have someone take you out for a jaunt. You hate staying in one place."

Funi shot him a look, gritting his teeth. "I was quite fine where I was, Refskegg. I've been… busy."

"Busy," Refskegg drawled. "Ah, yes; busy moping for the last two years."

Funi stubbornly turned his head away, and Refskegg sighed, hopping over to his friend's branch, and placing a hand on his shoulder.

"I can't imagine how you must feel right now, but it isn't healthy, what you've been doing. You're Austvindr; you need to feel the wind."

Funi was silent for a long moment before his shoulders slumped with a sigh. "I suppose you're right." He paused, then, his face screwing up in a scowl. "Did you have to take me to the Northland, though?"

"I'm afraid so," Refskegg said calmly. "Why do you ask?"

"The Old Man lives here!" Funi scowled.

"What's wrong with the Wanderer?" Refskegg's grinned, highly amused. "I've always found him to be quite the pleasant fellow."

"Of course, you would," his friend huffed indignantly. "You're cut from the same cloth, cunning tricksters that you are. As for me, whenever I'm in the area he spends his whole time teasing me!"

"Oh, does he?" Refskegg examined his fingers. "I hadn't noticed."

"My jewel, you haven't noticed, you old fox." Funi glared. "And it's gotten worse recently. Now he won't stop saying that he must be my hero. 'Imitation is the sincerest form of flattery' my foot!" He threw his hands in the air. "It had nothing to do with him! In fact, he was the exact furthest thing in my mind when it happened, the old—"

"Now, now, old friend," Refskegg cut in with a laugh. "It's not polite to insult our host."

Funi huffed but conceded the point. "Why did you bring me here, though?"

"Take a look," Refskegg replied, gesturing elegantly towards the clearing below them.

Funi grasped onto a nearby branch and leaned forward, peering down. After a moment a smile lit his face. "Is that young Flosi there? I wonder what he's doing here. Is that what you want me to see?"

"There was something amiss on this mountain," Refskegg said, leaning forward himself and looking down. "But it is gone now; I imagine his presence had something to do with that."

He paused thoughtfully, and when he spoke again his smile was sharp, his voice as sly and cunning as a fox. "It also might have something to do with the fact that little Ingirún's garden is nearby."

Funi grinned at this, but Refskegg cut him off with a wave of his hand. "But while that is certainly interesting, no, *that* is not why I brought you here. Look at the young man with the braids and see what he bears around his neck."

Funi looked down from his perch near the top of the ash tree's lofty height, eyeing the young man that Refskegg pointed out. After a moment, a quiet gasp left his lips. It was several minutes before he spoke again.

"I see." He said softly at last, a smile crossing his face. "Thank you for showing this to me. It's good to know where that little jewel of mine went, and that it lent its service to a good cause."

"Of course, my friend!" Refskegg replied. "I thought perhaps it might be a good thing to show you, now."

"Oh, is that so?" Funi raised one eyebrow. "And whyever would that be?"

"Ah, well…" Refskegg plucked a leaf from the branch before him, spinning it by the stem between his thumb and forefinger. "If I remember aright, that little bauble there was parted from you during a rather difficult situation in a somewhat… shall we say, painful manner?"

Funi's relaxed posture stiffened slightly, and a glare narrowed onto the form of his friend. "And so? What? Are you saying I should regret it?"

"Far be it from me to ever suggest such a thing," Refskegg replied, his voice grave. "No. I simply wanted to show you that that little stone there, cast into the wide world with pain and suffering… has found its own way to happiness and to bring happiness, just as you hoped for it. Even if it took a while."

There was a long silence, and the wind stirred through the branches; the leaves hushing gently against each other in a language only people such as those sitting in the tree could comprehend.

Finally, Funi's mouth slid into a smile, even if it had a slight hint of sadness in its shadow, and he dropped his head to rest in one hand. "… I see. Thank you, old friend. I'll keep that in mind."

Refskegg clapped his companion on the shoulder, and breathed a blessing onto the leaf, casting it onto the wind, which picked it up and gently carried it over and around each of the four people standing at the base of the ancient ash.

No one seemed to mark the fall of the leaf; no one, that is, save Flosi, who stared at it for a long while before glancing up, his eyes unerringly searching out the two hidden men.

After a long moment, Flosi smiled and lifted his hand in a wave, before turning his attention back to his fellows.

Refskegg smiled fondly down at the lad before returning his attention once more to his companion.

"No thanks are necessary," he said at last, his mouth curving into a sharp, answering grin. "That's what friends are for, are they not?"

They spent a great amount of time in the clearing, talking amongst themselves, but they could not stay there forever.

Svanhilda extended the hospitality of their home to their guests, which was gratefully accepted—even by Flosi.

"I shall have to be going soon," the bard had said thoughtfully, "now that my task is done. I shall replace the wards, but the immediate threat to the mirror is gone. It needn't be watched every waking moment, which means I am free to wander again. But," he said with a smile, "I confess I am not quite ready to quit your company, so I think I shall have to accept your offer." He lifted his head into the wind, closing his eyes and letting its song wash over him. "The wind ever calls, but I can tarry a little longer."

So, the five of them, along with Allvaldi, made their way to the house of Kiúli. Flosi had disappeared into the forest, being instructed to invite Eylir over for dinner, and Ásbjörn and Svanhilda had pulled ahead and were talking quietly between themselves.

Rósfrída lagged behind, for her legs were not used to much walking after seven years spent in one room. She was a far cry from the little girl who had climbed walls and run along the mountain slopes, but that was all right. That could be regained, now that she was free again!

Besides, Tryggvi kept pace with her, with Allvaldi trotting just ahead, so Rósfrída could not feel sorry for herself—not when she had such fine friends for company.

"I wonder…" she mused thoughtfully, and Tryggvi quirked a brow in question. "…I wonder if there is some sort of item out there, one with power, that would allow me to hear Allvaldi."

Allvaldi stopped in his tracks, turning around to face her. Rósfrída and Tryggvi stopped as well, and Rósfrída looked down, feeling her ears beginning to turn red.

"After all, he was able to hear me, and I would like very much to return the favor," she said, flushing even more.

Allvaldi gave her a long, slow look, his green eyes piercing her as if to plumb her depths.

Finally, he gave a sharp nod and turned to his human. *'I never thought I'd say this, but you have excellent taste. I approve this one.'*

Then he turned around, and continued his walk, but not before shooting one last word over his shoulder with a magnificent flick of his tail.

'Don't bungle it.'

Tryggvi stuck his tongue out at the cat's retreating back, causing Rósfrída to giggle quietly. "Do I even want to know?"

Tryggvi rubbed the back of his neck, fighting valiantly with the urge to blush. "He said a bunch of things, but it generally boils down to that he approves of you."

"Oh! Well, I'm flattered." She happily bounced a little. "I imagine Allvaldi is quite discerning when bestowing approval."

"Discerning is one word for it." Tryggvi rolled his eyes, before becoming thoughtful and returning to the original question. "Though, to answer your question… I don't know. I've never heard of an item like that."

Rósfrída's expression became downcast, but Tryggvi gently nudged her elbow with his and smiled. "Though, there are a great many things I've never heard of, and the world is wide indeed! I'm sure there's something like that out there; we just need to find it."

"Or find a smith with the skill to make such a thing!" she said excitedly. "That would be a fun adventure!"

"Do you like adventure?" Tryggvi asked curiously, taking her arm and helping her over a particularly tricky bit of terrain.

Rósfrída nodded enthusiastically. "Mama says I take after Papa; that I'm a child of the wind and sea. I always wanted to go and follow the wind where it wills." She sighed. "But then… well, you know. When I was in that room, I wanted to follow the wind even more than I had before; I guess because I knew I couldn't… But that's done and over with, now!" She closed her eyes, smiling brightly. "I can finally feel the wind and sun on my face again."

Tryggvi smiled down at her, and felt courage rise up in his heart, courage enough to speak. "If… if you think it over, my offer that is, and decide you will accept it—I'll take you wherever the wind blows, if you will."

Rósfrída opened her eyes and stared at him, before a slow smile began to curl across her face. "Do you mean that?"

Tryggvi nodded firmly, swallowing hard. "I do."

"Even West of the Moon and East of the Sun," she asked, raising her eyebrows in challenge, "like in the stories of Prince Býulfr?"

Tryggvi took her hand and raised it, pressing it gently to his heart, as if to let her feel his sincerity. "Even there." Then a grin split his face and his gray eyes twinkled with cloud-caught stars of mischief. "Though we might have to ask for directions."

A raven called loudly, and the Wanderer paused in the middle of the path, one eye peering up at the bird from beneath the brim of his hat. He stretched out his staff, and the raven flew down, landing delicately on the staff's end.

"How now, my friend," the Wanderer said. "What news do you have for me this day?"

He listened for a long time, nodding along here and there, and finally, a slow smile spread across his face.

"I thank you, my friend," he said solemnly, and gifted the bird with a small strip of jerky. "You may return."

The raven called out once more and then rose, mighty wings carrying it swiftly away.

The Wanderer watched it go, slowly stroking a hand down his beard, his one eye twinkling.

"Well," he said, "that's taken care of. The girl is freed, and the boy as well; and the pelt I gifted long ago can once more be used as a blessing rather than a curse."

He sighed, but it was a happy sigh—a sigh of delight. "All's well that ends well, as they say. And I for one am very fond of happy endings."

He faced Westward and tipped his hat towards Alvíss' mountain, but then turned away, and continued his slow walk along the mountain path. He was the Wanderer, after all, whose spear stood guard for all the children of the Northlands: for those of forest, and mountain, and the sea-wind.

The shadows that clung to the mountain of Alvíss had been driven away and now were no more; it was time to seek out others in need of happiness.

Epilogue

Mama," Dagný said, skipping into the house and plopping herself down at the foot of her mother's chair, "can you pack me a lunch?"

Queen Ljúfvina set down her sewing, somewhat surprised. Dagný often went out on picnic lunches when Tryggvi was here, but in the three weeks he'd been gone, she'd refused to do so.

"It's not the same without Tryggvi," she'd insisted, and ate in front of the fire, sneaking tidbits to Frode instead.

So this came as a bit of a surprise. However, Ljúfvina was an experienced mother, and swiftly rose to the occasion. "Of course, dear," she said, and got up to begin packing a satchel. "What's brought this on, though?"

Dagný frowned thoughtfully, swirling her finger through the fur of the bearskin rug. "I don't know." She shrugged. "I just have a feeling today's gonna be a good day."

Ljúfvina smiled at her fondly and wrapped a piece of cheese in a cloth and tucked it in the satchel. "Well, I hope you have a lovely day, then." She looked over her shoulder at her daughter and quirked a brow. "Is Frode going to be eating with you?"

Dagný nodded firmly, her eyes wide in a way that communicated she thought that was a question with an obvious answer.

Ljúfvina merely smiled and packed plenty of extra venison.

When the satchel was ready, Dagný hugged her mother and took the satchel, bolting out the door.

Frode was sitting on the grass outside and Dagný crouched down next to him, scratching behind his ears. "C'mon, Frode, it's lunch time, and we're having a picnic at the gate!"

Frode hauled himself up and stretched with a mighty yawn but trotted slowly after Dagný.

The little princess ran through the streets, waving to people as she went, but she didn't stop. She ran right up to the gate of the town and sat down in the middle of it. She took her satchel in her lap and opened it up. She tore a piece of venison in two and handed one half to Frode, who snapped it up eagerly. The other she slowly sucked on, eyes fixed on the road.

She wasn't quite sure where the feeling came from, but she *knew* it, deep in her bones. Something good would happen today, and Dagný was pretty sure she knew what it was going to be.

She'd been sitting there for several hours, picking slowly at her picnic lunch to make it last, when Frode slowly stood up. He stared, then slowly his tail began to wag, going faster and faster.

Dagný looked up from nibbling her current piece of cheese, curious to see what had caught her dog's attention—and then she saw it herself.

Two men were walking down the road. The one with the great white pelt about his shoulders she did not recognize, but the other, the one with a golden cat trotting at his side—she would know him anywhere.

Frode let out a loud, sharp bark, and burst into a run. It was a little stiff and shambling, as Frode was no longer the puppy that had been left to guard a boy ten years before, but he didn't let that stop him.

Dagný let out a gasp and scrambled to her feet, running after him, her hair streaming behind her in the wind like a tongue of flame. The two men saw her and her dog running, and they broke into a sprint too. The stretch of road between them shrank, and shrank, and then it was gone. Dagný flung herself into Tryggvi's arms, and the man with the white pelt had sunk onto his knees to receive a jubilant dog.

Tryggvi caught his little sister neatly, quite used to this greeting, and swung her around, both of them laughing.

Frode was shivering with joy, yipping and barking, his tail stirring up a breeze as he tried to lick every inch of his master's face.

"See, Dagný?" Tryggvi said, shifting his hold on her and turning to Ásbjörn. "I kept my promise. I brought brother Ásbjörn back, just as I said I would."

Dagný nodded solemnly, staring down at Ásbjörn with wide eyes even as she leaned to whisper in Tryggvi's ear. "I knew you'd bring him back."

Tryggvi smiled and hugged her just a little bit tighter.

At this, Ásbjörn gave Frode one last ear scratch and stood up, locking gazes with Dagný. She looked back at him shyly, biting her lip.

Ásbjörn smiled gently, his eyes bright with emotion. "You know, I've always wanted a little sister. I'm very glad to have met you, Dagný. Can I be your brother?"

Dagný's eyes widened, and she glanced back at Tryggvi, who smiled and nodded. She turned back to Ásbjörn and nodded firmly, reaching out towards him.

Ásbjörn, whose big brother skills had not dulled in the slightest, knew what she wanted. He reached back toward her, and Tryggvi carefully transferred his burden into Ásbjörn's arms.

Once there, Dagný flung her arms about Ásbjörn's neck and pulled herself up high enough to shyly press a kiss to his bearded cheek. "Love you, big brother."

Ásbjörn smiled and leaned his cheek against the top of her head, hugging her close. "And I love you."

"And I love you both!" Tryggvi exclaimed, wrapping his arms around them. "And Allvaldi does too, though he'd never admit it."

Allvaldi lifted his nose and flicked his tail as if to show what he thought of such a statement, but it is notable that he, for once, had nothing to say.

Sounds of footsteps reached them then, pounding frantically against the dirt, and they looked up.

When Dagný had gone running out from the gate, the gatekeeper had sent word to the king and queen, announcing that Prince Tryggvi had returned.

So the King and Queen had rushed to the edge of the city to welcome him home, never guessing that Tryggvi wasn't alone.

But he wasn't—and though Ásbjörn had grown and changed, they saw him, and they *knew.*

Ljúfvina reached them first, for nothing is more swift than a mother's love, and she slammed into the group, her arms reaching to encompass them all as she burst into sobs. Ólaf was just behind her, however, and he somehow managed to sweep them all up in his grip and lift them off the ground, his chest booming with a strange mix of sobbing and laughter.

Finally, however, they were all set back on their feet, though they all still huddled close together, and Dagný arms couldn't be pried from around Ásbjörn's neck.

Ásbjörn looked at them:

At his father, whose hair was more gray than orange now, but still as strong and tall as ever.

At his mother, who had lines of sorrow about the corners of her eyes and mouth, but who was still lovely as the snow on the mountain, and whose eyes shone brightly with love.

At Tryggvi, who had grown into a man, tall and strong, laughing and kind; yet he was still Ásbjörn's little brother, as he ever had been.

At Dagný, who was entirely new to him, but precious and lovely and loved; his sweet little sister to cherish, a gift from the Highest Heaven.

At Frode, who had known him as a bear, and who knew him now years and years later, his tail thumping the ground in happiness.

At Allvaldi, who was watching the reunion smugly, as if he himself had orchestrated the entire affair.

Ásbjörn looked at his family, and he smiled.

"I know I'm a bit late," he said, "but I've come home again."

>>*<< · >>*<< · >>*<<

Kiúli stopped in front of the door of his house, his shoulders slumped under the heavy burden of failure.

He'd been gone on this latest trip for months, scouring the trading towns for something, *anything*, that might be able to help his little girl. But, as always, he'd found nothing.

And now he'd returned, empty handed.

Now he'd have to watch the hope bleed out of his wife's eyes, replaced by the too-familiar sorrow. He'd do anything to never have to see that look again.

Still, he couldn't stay on his threshold forever, so with a heavy sigh, he opened the door and stepped inside. His shoulders were still slumped, and his head bowed, as if to stave off the sight of the inevitable sadness and despair.

He closed the door behind him and only then raised his head—and he stopped in his tracks and stared.

He saw his wife, practically glowing with happiness and rounded with a child he hadn't known was there; a child that would soon be born—a little boy who would love the sea winds, just like his father.

He saw his eldest daughter, beaming and content in a way he hadn't seen in years, and wearing fine jewelry that he had never bought her, jewelry carved with the bear of the Björnings.

But in this moment, he hardly noticed any of that—for there was his little daughter; not so little any longer, but a woman grown—sweet and lovely and *free*.

In the next moment, his arms were full of his girls, all three of them; and he buried his face in his wife's hair and felt grateful tears trace down his cheeks.

Rósfríða was home again.

The End

ACKNOWLEGDMENTS

As always, thanks go to the Frosty Sisters: Cortney, Cathrine, Sarah, and Kendra, for all their fellowship and support. Special gratitude is dedicated to Kendra and Sarah, whose help was invaluable in the effort to get this book out in time.

To my best buddies: Katie and Rebeka, for their electronic hugs and ever-present cheering from the wings. Your support is invaluable, and I can't express how many times you've cheered me up and given me the strength I need to get more words out and come up with exciting plot twists; and to Hannah, for being a good friend, an inspiration, and a very cool person overall.

To all my family: My cousin Ana-Marie, whose enthusiasm for my stories is always an encouragement and inspiration; to my new sister, Molly, and her sister, Erin, for all their prayers and support; and to Meredith for all your encouragement. My brothers, for their thoughts, prayers, and help; with special thanks going to Tryg, for both being so kind as to let me name a character after him and for reading through it himself to give me feedback; and Caedmon for help with formatting and for Rick Rolling me with the chapter links.

To Dad: for his belief both in my skills and that I'd get things done quicker if I didn't procrastinate so much.

To Mom: who has dedicated so much time and aid to helping me get this book out; so much so that I can never repay it.

To my family as a whole: who taught me what a good family looks like, so I know how to write good families in my stories.

ABOUT THE AUTHOR

Wyn Estelle Owens is the penname of a young woman who's still figuring out what this whole 'adult' thing is all about. She lives in a big, old house in Maryland by a Hundred Acre Wood (dubbed Neldoreth) with her parents, two occasionally obnoxious brothers, her dog Jackie, and her personal plot bunny, Joker.

She is fond of reading, writing, drawing, speaking in dead or imaginary languages, playing videogames, quoting classic or obscure literature, being randomly dramatic, and generally making things out of yarn. Her dream is to write stories that inspire people to chase after the wonderful world of storytelling.

Her favorite all-time authors are Anne Elisabeth Stengl and especially J.R.R. Tolkien, who first inspired her to pursue novel writing when she read *The Hobbit* at the age of seven.

www.ingramcontent.com/pod-product-compliance
Lightning Source LLC
Chambersburg PA
CBHW052004150726
47999CB00004B/1515